Marie's
HIDDEN REFUGE

DANIELLE M HAAS

Cover created by Deranged Doctor Designs.

A Danielle M Haas Publishing Book

Marie's Hidden Refuge - Safe Haven Women's Shelter

To Lewis, the grandfather I always wanted and will always love. The greatest Pappy to my children. The light who will always live on in all of us.

A NOTE TO THE READER

To my wonderful reader,

Thank you so much for choosing to read Marie's Hidden Refuge. Before you begin, I wanted to let you know this book contains a story about a strong woman who has survived her abusive ex. The book contains themes of domestic abuse.

If you or anyone you know finds yourself in an abusive situation and you need someone to talk to, please call the National Domestic Violence Hotline at 1-800-799-SAFE (1-800-799-7233).

1

Heavy vibrations from the old washing machine slammed against the concrete floor and roused Marie from a deep sleep. She blinked in rapid succession to clear the fog from her mind and took in the sights of the small living room. The rough material of the threadbare couch scraped against the exposed skin of her legs and the smell of stale cigarettes assaulted her senses.

Nora was snuggled tightly in her bassinet beside her, fast asleep. Deep, all-consuming love tightened her chest, followed by a quick stab of guilt. Her two-month-old daughter was the only bright spot in her life but raising her in such a crappy environment weighed heavy on Marie's shoulders.

A quick glance at the digital clock on the glass television stand told her the bars would close soon. A shiver ran down her spine despite the stifling heat in the run-down bungalow she shared with her ex-boyfriend. Bill would be home soon and if she had to tell him one more thing was broken in the hellhole they called a home, he wouldn't be happy.

The bruise he'd left on her jaw from the night before throbbed at the possibility of his reaction.

A small cry curled Nora's lips, and she kicked her legs free of her swaddle.

Clamoring to her feet, Marie pushed a strand of dark hair from her face and hurried to pick her up before heading to the laundry room at the back of the house. The washer hopped across the cement, beating harder and faster against the floor, its desperate cries for attention echoing through the room. Marie lunged for the machine and quickly turned it off.

Tears gathered at the corners of her eyes, and she leaned against the now dormant machine. How had she let her life come to this? Throwing in a load of wash while Bill got drunk so he wouldn't be upset she forgot to clean his clothes? Running to the laundry room in the middle of the night to turn off a broken washer so Bill wouldn't come home from the bar angry?

It had to end. Sucking in a deep breath, she searched for the courage to leave. Her options may be limited—heck, they were close to non-existent—but she couldn't put it off any longer. A life lived in fear—placing her baby in danger—wasn't a life she wanted to live anymore. Even if it meant putting her mom at risk of going back to jail.

The sound of the screen door banging against the side of the house set Marie's nerves on edge. Bill's rough, loud voice raised the hairs on her arm. A giggle tickled her eardrum. Marie straightened and held her breath, straining her ears toward the front of the house. Mumbled voices penetrated the thin walls. A humorless laugh puffed from her mouth.

He brought another woman home?

Enough was enough. She couldn't wait a second longer to get out of this house and away from the man she'd been forced to leave her hometown with. An image of the notebook she kept tucked under her mattress sprang to mind, and she cringed. She needed her notes, and the small amount of money she'd managed to hide, but no way she could walk past Bill to get her things then march out the door.

The voices grew louder, closer, and Marie's heart raced. She glanced around, but there was nowhere to hide. The laundry room barely held enough space for their machines, and if Bill stepped into the kitchen, there'd be no way he wouldn't see her.

Crack!

Marie lifted her palm to her face. She'd been slapped enough times to know that sound, and images of how alcohol fueled Bill's treatment of a woman when he was drunk and wanted satisfied filled her brain. Silence occupied the house for a brief second then angry voices exploded, heavy footsteps pounding her way. Fear churned in her gut. She had to get out of here—now. It didn't matter that she had nothing more than the clothes on her back and no place to stay. A night in the woods was better than the hell waiting for her here.

Than the hell waiting for her innocent daughter.

Summoning whatever bravery Bill hadn't managed to destroy, Marie found her baby carrier on top of the dryer and strapped a sleeping Nora to her chest. She tip-toed toward the back door. The coolness of the cement seeped into her bare feet, but at least it didn't shift with her every step. Slipping into the flip-flops she'd left beside the door, she bit into her bottom lip and gently pushed open the old door.

The rusted hinges creaked with the motion, and every muscle in her body tensed. The yelling continued behind her, covering the noise. She swung the door open wider and a high-pitched scream followed by a loud *thud* froze Marie's blood and stole her ability to move. Her instinct screamed to check on the woman, but she couldn't put Nora in danger.

She had to run.

Hurrying through the door, she darted toward the thick foliage that kept her house hidden from the rest of the inhabitants of the small Tennessee town where she and Bill had recently relocated. She flew from the concrete stoop, one palm firmly holding Nora in place, and floodlights from atop the battered roof illuminated the backyard.

Dread threatened to stall her. No way Bill hadn't seen the flash of light through the front window. She sprinted toward the darkened tree line at the edge of their property, and soon the long blades of grass scraped against her calves. Moisture from the earlier rain clung to her skin. Her chest tightened with every step, every ragged breath, every fearful thought of what Bill would do to her and Nora if he caught them.

Lengthening her stride, she ducked under low branches and weaved between trees. She sped down the hill that led to the river, and her heels skidded on loose leaves covering the ground. She wrapped her hand around the rough bark of a nearby tree and steadied herself. Energy leaked from her pores, but she pushed forward, using tree after tree for support against her weakening limbs. Time slipped by in a haze—seconds morphing into minutes and minutes ticking into a blur.

The snapping of twigs behind her rang out like cannon fire in the warm night air. Nora's steady breathing told her that her sweet baby was oblivious to the danger around them. Sweat trickled through the damp hair matted at Marie's temple, and sharp spasms of pain pierced her side, but she had to keep moving—had to keep running. If he caught her, he'd kill her.

Lord only knew what he'd do to Nora.

Booted footsteps pounded the wooded ground behind her, and she chanced a quick glance over her shoulder. Shadows moved between the trees, but the blanket of clouds across the moonless sky made it impossible to make out the monster stalking her.

Facing forward again, a light on the top of the riverbank

flicked on. Indecision slowed her footsteps. Her options were low. She could run to the water or trust a stranger.

Decision made, she turned toward the light and stumbled forward, struggling not to wake the baby. Her thighs burned as she clamored up the slight incline. A low growl sounded behind her. Not a bear or a dog, but a deep feral growl of a man possessed. Swallowing her fear, she gathered all her strength and ran up the hill. Her foot caught on a root, and she fell to her knees. Jagged stones sliced the flesh that her jean shorts didn't protect, but she couldn't slow down.

"You'll never escape me." Bill hissed through the dark.

A tremor shook her hands the way it always did when Bill was too close. She clawed through the mud and loose pebbles and tried to get to her feet. She shifted to the side to protect Nora from the impact of the ground.

A hand tightened around her ankle and pulled her down the hill.

"I need to teach you a lesson." Bill's harsh laugh vibrated through the trees and birds scattered into the night.

Tears stung her eyes, and she glanced toward the light—toward the freedom she would never know. Darkness moved into the center of the beacon of hope she once had, light still seeping around the image taking shape. She blinked, trying to bring the shadow into focus, but it was no use.

Bang!

A gunshot cut through the air, and she flinched, hurrying to cover Nora's ears. The pressure around her ankle released, and she scurried forward.

She didn't look back, just focused on the light and whatever angel had been sent to help her. She neared the top of the hill and slowed her pace. Her heart beat an erratic rhythm in her chest. Nora woke and a piercing cry erupted from her tiny lungs. "Shhh, baby girl. It's okay. We're going to be okay."

Standing above her at the top of the hill was an old man weathered by time. Deep wrinkles rippled across his forehead and strands of what was left of his wiry white hair whipped along with the subtle breeze. His firm stance and piercing blue eyes told her not to underestimate his small stature.

"Come on, girl. Get on up here. We need to take care of that little bundle." He lowered his rifle to his side and started back toward his house.

She darted her gaze around the backyard, but nothing lingered except a black cat sleeping on the railing of the porch. The old man stepped through the back door of his small brick house and left the door wide open. She glanced behind her, but darkness swallowed whatever laid hidden in the trees.

Is Bill dead?

She couldn't waste time finding out. She filled her lungs with air, summoned all of her strength, and ran for the house. She didn't know who this old man was, but one thing was certain, he'd just saved her life.

OWEN WELLS STOOD outside his grandfather's house and took in the splintered old wood of the front porch. Pulled-down shades covered the windows, obscuring the inside of the house from anyone lurking outside. The warm morning sun had yet to dry the drops of dew from on top of the splintered railing of the porch, but no doubt the pleasant beams of light beating down on him would soon bring the blistering May heat before noon.

Sweat already clung to the small of his back, and mud splattered up his pant legs. Starting his day on the banks of the river at the crack of dawn hadn't been fun, especially when the reason for dragging him there was murder.

A shudder ripped through him. He'd been a sheriff's deputy for the last seven years, and he'd never witnessed the bloated face of death like he had today. Hell, he'd lived in Water's Edge, Tennessee, his entire life and could only recall three murders. But none had washed up on the shores of the river when he was the one in charge of finding the killer.

Loose pebbles crunched beneath his boots as he closed the distance between his truck and the house. The familiar pang of guilt sliced through him. He hadn't been here in months, but that's the way his grandpa liked it—isolated and alone with only his constant need for answers to keep him company.

But he couldn't respect the walls his grandpa had put up now. He had answers of his own to find, and if he were lucky, his grandpa's neurotic habits might give him some of the insight he needed.

The ancient wood groaned beneath him as he stood in front of the dirty white storm door. He pulled the black handle, and snorted when the locked door didn't budge.

Most people in these parts didn't lock their doors, but his grandpa was the exception to the rule. Fisting his hand, he knocked on the door and waited. Seconds ticked by, and the whoosh of cars on the main road leading outside of town sounded behind him.

"Come on, Old Man. I know you're awake. Answer the door." He rapped his knuckles again. No one stood on Lewis Sinclair's porch without him knowing about it, no matter what time of day.

The door swung open, forcing Owen to take a step back.

"What are you doing here?" Lewis pulled down his thin lips in a frown, but he couldn't hide the twinkle in his blue eyes whenever Owen came around.

No matter how much Pappy grumbled about not wanting any company, he could never hide his secret pleasure at spending time with his grandkids. "I need to talk to you. Can I come in?"

"Fine. But don't expect me to offer you breakfast." Lewis turned his back and walked into the shadows of the house.

Owen snorted out a laugh and followed him inside, closing the door behind him. The stilted air inside the house engulfed him. "Want me to open a window for you, Pappy? It's hot as Hades in here."

Lewis waved his hand as he passed through the threshold to the kitchen, disappearing from view.

Owen sighed. He should have known better than offer a suggestion. Best to get this over with. He had too much work to waste time. He crossed the woven oval rug in the living room, following his grandpa's path into the next room. "Do you still have the cameras in your backyard? The ones you use to watch the woods? There was an incident—"

A young woman with her eyes cast toward her lap at the oak table halted his train of thought, a baby nestled in her arms. His grandpa sat beside her, a cup of coffee with wisps of steam spiraling into the air in front of him.

Owen tore his gaze from the dark-haired woman with long matted hair falling down her back and small scrapes dashed across her cheeks. His grandpa having any company at his home was odd, but especially a beautiful woman and a baby. "I didn't know you had company."

Lewis took a sip of coffee then stared at Owen. "You never asked. Now what brings you by so early?"

Pulling out a chair, Owen fought not to dart his gaze to the stranger in the corner.

He sat and scratched his whiskered chin, needing to weigh his words carefully in front of the unexpected visitor. "I need to look at the video feed of the cameras you have in the backyard."

Lewis tilted his head and cradled his hands around the mug. "Why?"

Owen cleared his throat and chanced a glance at the woman before returning his gaze to his grandpa. The young woman may be beautiful, and the little one with the large green eyes cute as hell, but he didn't want to speak about an active investigation in front of her. He also wanted to ask his grandpa who she was and why she sat in his kitchen first thing in the morning. "Can we speak privately?"

"Nope. Spill it."

Owen clenched his jaw and silently cursed the old man's stubbornness. "A jogger stumbled across a crime scene this morning. Your cameras might have something on them I can use."

A sharp gasp sounded, and Owen stared at the wide green eyes—eyes so much like her child's—of the mystery woman.

"I'm sorry. We haven't been introduced. I'm Owen, a deputy for the local sheriff's department." He extended his hand across the four-person table and waited for the girl to take it.

She moistened her lips and shifted her gaze toward Lewis for a brief second, then took Owen's hand before resting it on her child's back, her gaze following suit. "Marie. This is Nora."

The ugly bruise along Marie's jaw raised his blood pressure. Owen waited a beat but wasn't rewarded with more than the breathy name that barely escaped her pouty mouth.

"Now you've met. Tell me how my video feed could be of any use." Lewis spoke quickly, demanding Owen's attention.

Fine. If the old man wanted him to be blunt, he'd be blunt. "A dead body was found washed ashore on the river a little bit south of here. Foul play is suspected. Thanks to your paranoia and extensive property along the river, you have cameras that could have caught vital information to the investigation. Chances are I can get a warrant. Better to let me look now than wait for the sheriff to get involved. We both know that wouldn't be a good idea."

Red invaded Lewis' normally pale cheeks, and he tightened

his grip around his mug. "I don't want your father anywhere near me or my stuff."

Raising to his feet, Owen ran a hand through his hair and made his way to the coffee pot. He hated using his father's name to get what he wanted, but pushing that particular button was the best way to get his grandpa to fold.

Owen grabbed a coffee mug from the cabinet and used the half-empty pot to fill his cup. He brought the cup to his lips, and the bitter black liquid burned his tongue. The pain kept him from saying something he'd regret. He turned back toward the table, and a shotgun by the back door caught his eye. Placing the mug down on the Formica counter, he marched to the gun and turned hard eyes on his grandpa. "What's this doing here?"

"It's my fault, not his." Marie stood, the back of her chair colliding against the wall, and faced him. "He helped me. He saved me."

The moisture in her green eyes was the like dew clinging to the long blades of grass in the front yard and only heightened the queasiness eating away at his stomach lining. His first instinct was to calm Marie and promise her everything was fine, but her words needed to be explored. Something wasn't right.

"Sit down, girl." Lewis placed a hand on her arm and coaxed her back in the chair.

"You can sit, but you need to tell me what's going on. How did my grandpa save you when he barely ever leaves his house?"

A shuddering breath raised Marie's shoulders. "I needed to get away. I didn't have a choice. If your grandpa wouldn't have shot at Bill, he would have killed me."

Confusion and dread collided in Owen's brain. "Who's Bill?"

"My...roommate." Hesitation slowed her speech. "Isn't he the person who was found dead?"

"No. An unidentified woman was found this morning." Owen pinched the bridge of his nose and returned to his seat, leaving his coffee on the counter. His stomach couldn't handle the extra acid right now. "But you need to tell me who Bill is and why my grandfather might have shot him."

2

Marie fell into the hard, wooden chair and fought to keep her rising panic from sucking her into its vortex. She cradled Nora tighter to her chest then kissed her soft head. Bill wasn't dead. Someone else had been found. How was that possible? Bill wouldn't have released his grip on her if he hadn't been hurt. No way he would have just let her walk away.

If he wasn't dead, he wouldn't stop looking for her. Wouldn't stop looking for his daughter.

The man across from her—Owen—cleared his throat, breaking into her spiraling thoughts. She glanced at him, and the shafts of light pouring through the windows crashed into her eyes. Bits of dust floated through the beams. Not surprising since a film appeared to cover most of the items inside Lewis' home.

She shifted to avoid the harsh rays and tried to calm her racing heart. Blinking, she brought Owen's scruffy cheeks and sharp hazel eyes into focus. All the moisture in her mouth evaporated, but she couldn't be sure if it was from fear over

Bill's unknown fate or her unexpected attraction for the deputy. "Can I get some water?"

Owen kept his narrowed gaze on her face, and heat engulfed her cheeks.

"You heard her, get the girl a glass of water," Lewis said, his words grumbling from his throat.

Owen strolled to the cabinet to grab a tall glass then fill it with water from the faucet.

Marie couldn't help the small curve of her lips. Lewis barked out orders to his grandson as if he spoke to a child, not a full-grown adult who stopped by for information about an investigation.

A chill swept over her despite the suffocating heat in the small kitchen. A dead body that needed to be investigated meant only one thing—the woman from the night before had been murdered.

Owen sat back down and slid a clear glass across the table. She reached for it and her fingers brushed against his, sending a ripple of excitement through her body. Yanking back her hand, she smoothed her palm over Nora's soft curls and dropped her gaze to the edge of the rounded table. She needed to keep a level head right now, not get lost in a stupid fantasy about a handsome deputy sent from heaven to save her. Real life had provided her with enough heartache, she didn't need to set herself up for disappointment in her daydreams as well. Besides, one thing she'd learned long ago, the only person she could depend on to save her was herself.

"You gonna drink the water, or what?" Lewis chuckled and clicked his tongue.

"Marie," Owen said, reclaiming her attention with his velvety smooth voice. "I need to know why you're here."

"That's none of your business, boy. You want the video feed from my cameras, fine. But there's no need to drag this poor girl into your mess." Lewis pushed up from the table and stormed out of the kitchen.

Marie bit into her top lip and darted her gaze between the two men. Trouble was the last thing she wanted to start, but the tension buzzing in the room reminded her of the time she'd stumbled upon a hornet's nest.

Owen watched Lewis until he disappeared into the shadows then turned his full attention on her. "He's a stubborn old man, always has been. But if he shot someone, I need to know. You said he helped you last night, now let me help him. Tell me what happened."

Her mind spun. Lewis had saved hers and Nora's lives and given them shelter. She didn't want to cause him grief. But if Bill was out there, she needed someone on her side, and someone with a badge could be the ticket she needed to finally be free of a man she despised.

The only problem lay in what Bill would do if arrested. She'd entered into their arrangement to protect her sister—and keep her mom out of jail—but if Bill were threatened by the authorities, all of the sacrifices she'd made could be for nothing.

Not to mention the risk of him fighting for custody over Nora. She'd rather live the rest of her life under his abusive thumb than be forced to leave her baby with him.

Unless they had enough to put him behind bars.

Marie took a sip of water and let the cool liquid slide down her throat. Setting the glass aside, she straightened her spine and rested her gaze on Owen's broad shoulders, unable to retell the events of the previous night while looking into his eyes. "The man I live with—Bill—came home drunk from the bar last night. He has a temper, and when alcohol's involved, it's always worse."

"Is he responsible for the bruise on your jaw?"

The kindness in his voice lifted her gaze to his and

squeezed her heart. She'd never reported the violence she'd suffered at Bill's hand, but if she were going to confide in this man, she might as well confess it all. "Yes." The word croaked from her still-dry throat, and she took another sip of water.

Owen shifted in his seat and moved his clenched jaw from side to side. "So, you left after he hit you?"

She dropped her gaze again. "No. He hit me two nights ago. I left because he brought home another woman, and he hit her. I needed to get Nora out of there."

"Geez," Owen muttered.

A heavy *thump* on the table made Marie jump in her seat. She glanced up to find Lewis glowering at his grandson.

"Leave her out of this."

Owen sighed. "Pappy, I need to figure out what kind of mess you got yourself involved in, and I don't have time to waste."

Lewis nodded toward the tapes he'd tossed on the table. "You got what you came for. Go do your job, boy."

"I'm trying to do my job." Owen shot to his feet and towered over the older man.

Lewis jabbed a finger at Owen's chest. "Your job doesn't concern her, that baby, me or anything that happened here last night."

Marie flinched, waiting for tempers to boil over.

Leaning forward, Owen gently curled his palm around Lewis' bicep. "If you shot a man, I need to understand why. Then I need to find him."

Owen's tenderness melted her bones. She'd never witnessed a man use a calm hand and a steady voice instead of raised fists and shouting.

With Nora snug in her arms, Marie hoisted herself from the chair and both men studied her. "Lewis, I appreciate you saving me last night, but he's right. I don't want you to get in trouble because of me."

Lewis snorted, and Owen silenced him with a hard look.

Marie sucked in a deep breath, needing to press forward. "I ran away, and Bill followed. He caught my ankle and pulled me to the ground. He would have killed me, and probably Nora, for running. Lewis showed up, shot his gun, and Bill released his grip. I didn't have anywhere else to go."

Tears filled her eyes, but she blinked them away. This old man hadn't only saved her and her baby's lives, he'd shown her the first act of kindness she'd experienced in a long time.

Owen rubbed the back of his neck. "Did you look in the woods? Check to see if he's there?"

"Hell no," Lewis barked. "I wasn't about to traipse through the woods in the middle of the night. If the guy bled out in the woods, he deserved worse. I called the cops, who went over to their house and didn't find anyone."

"I need to check the woods. Can you show me where you were?" Owen dropped his hand and turned for the back door.

"Straight down the hill. Can't miss it." Lewis sat and grabbed his mug.

Owen glanced over his shoulder. "Seriously? You won't come outside and show me?"

Lewis shrugged and sipped his coffee.

"I'll show you," Marie said.

Owen turned concerned eyes her way. "Are you sure?"

She wasn't sure of anything, but she couldn't admit that. If she wanted a different life, she had to do something to make it happen. Showing Owen the spot where she'd struggled was the first step. And hopefully, the steps after would lead to finding Bill and help put him in prison where he belonged.

She could only pray that turning her back on Bill wouldn't mean condemning the rest of her family in the process.

OWEN FOLLOWED Marie out the door. She didn't slow her gait to wait for him, even with a baby strapped to her chest. He had so many questions for the mysterious young woman, but her abrupt pace across the yard made it clear she didn't want his company.

He fisted his hands at his sides as he trailed behind her. The nasty bruise along her jaw made him want to find the bastard she lived with and do much worse to him—if the man wasn't dead already. She'd appeared timid when he'd first walked into his grandpa's kitchen, but now she walked with her head held high and determination in her long strides.

The heat had already intensified in the brief time Owen had been inside his grandpa's house, causing beads of sweat to form along his hairline. He wanted to get this mess figured out and get back to identifying the woman who'd been found dead in the river that morning. No identification had been located on the body, and he hadn't received a call from Tommy about cause of death.

He fought the urge to call his little brother. Dumb luck had brought Tommy to the crime scene after the jogger called the station. His brother hadn't been on the job more than a handful of months, and he'd been the first on scene for a crime no one on their small department was prepared for.

The familiar pang of over-protectiveness tempted Owen to keep Tommy away from the investigation, but the limited resources at his disposal didn't make that a possibility. Besides, Tommy needed to be thrown into the deep end to see if he'd swim.

But first he had to figure out what his grandpa had done.

Tension built between his eyes with every step toward the hill at the end of the property. The tall trees provided a canopy of shade against the blistering heat.

Marie stopped, and he allowed himself one more glance at her tight backside and lean legs—both on full display in her short jean shorts. The muscles in his stomach tightened before he finally averted his gaze and came to a stop beside her.

Marie pointed down the hill. "I think we were right down there."

"You think?"

She shrugged and wrapped her arms around her sleeping baby. "It was dark, and I was scared. I can't be completely sure. We just moved to the area, and I don't even know where I am or how far I ran last night."

"Stay here. I'll walk down and see if I find anything."

He stomped down the hill, careful not to skid on the still-damp grass. Clumps of dried mud and tattered lawn told of a desperate attempt to get up the hill. The rain from the previous day would have made the slick ground more difficult to traverse. He imaged Marie running for her life, and anger heated his blood. Thank God his grandpa had been outside to help her, but hopefully his assistance to a woman he didn't know hadn't turned him into a killer.

A large imprint on pushed-down grass caught his attention a few yards down. He scanned the ground as he made his way toward the area, searching for any signs of an injured man. Broken twigs and loose leaves scattered around, but nothing out of the ordinary. He moved slowly down the hill and a splash of red stood out against the green grass pressed against the forest floor.

Crouching, he studied the stains. Large pools of blood splattered the area, trailing into dots of crimson toward the river.

"Did you find anything?" Marie called from the top of the hill.

"Blood. I'm gonna follow the trail and see where it takes me. Looks like to the river, but you never know what I might find." Owen took slow steps down the hill, making sure to take in as much of the area as possible.

The rustle of grass sounded behind him, and he turned and watched Marie make her way down the hill. Beams of light threaded through the leaf-filled branches and bounced around her, illuminating the beauty of her natural complexion and highlighting her willowy frame. Stands of dark hair snagged along branches, and she swatted at gnats as she walked toward him, pausing for a brief moment to stare at the blood that probably belonged to her boyfriend or whatever he was.

"You can head back to my grandpa's. You don't need to see this." As much as he'd love to get to know more about Marie, being in the woods searching for an injured and possibly dangerous man wasn't a safe place for her or her child.

She shook her head and darted her gaze up the hill toward the other side of the river. "No. I'd rather go with you."

Owen tracked more blood to the edge of the shallow river. The water barely skimmed the top of his ankles, giving him a clear view of the muddy bottom. Tinges of crimson speckled along the mud, turning to face North, until disappearing completely in the water.

Someone had tracked a lot of blood through the woods, but at least another dead body didn't litter the shore.

"Would Bill go home if he were hurt or call for help?"

"Home if he had a choice. He doesn't trust many people, especially here."

"I need to walk a little further. You mentioned not knowing how long you ran last night. Where exactly is your house?" Owen had racked his brain since she'd mentioned her escape. His grandpa lived on the main road out of town, and his property ran along for miles.

If Marie had ran out of her house and straight into the woods and ended up in Lewis' backyard, her house couldn't be too far away. Which either meant her home sat on land she didn't own, or she had run a lot further than he'd originally thought.

Marie shrugged. "I live a mile or so out of town. We've only been here about a month. I don't even know the house number. But the house is surrounded by woods, not visible from the main road. I couldn't have gone too far."

Owen stepped carefully along the muddy banks. Dread settled in the pit of his stomach. Chances were Marie and Bill were squatting on his grandpa's property. Trespassers often crossed the edges of the old man's land, but his grandpa was too consumed with his own demons to care. Owen had tried to patrol the property and keep the woods clear, but he'd let that chore slip over the past few years.

Silence settled between him and Marie, the only sound the chattering of birds and scampering of critters among the trees. Owen kept his gaze on the ground and his ears tuned into anything that could clue him in to where Bill might be.

Time slipped by little by little and some of the tension fell from his shoulders. He might have a suspicious death to investigate and a missing person with a possible gunshot wound, but nothing calmed his frayed nerves like being in the quiet of nature. He could almost trick himself into believing he was enjoying a Monday morning stroll in the woods with a beautiful woman and even cuter baby.

A streak of blood ran up the hill, and Owen crouched beside it. Dried blood stained the mud and smeared a path up the hill. No body littered the ground, but a new trail led back up to what he assumed was Marie's home. He followed the path like a bloodhound with a scent, glancing behind him to make sure Marie kept up on the steep incline.

At the top of the hill a clearing appeared, leaving enough space for a small house tucked deep within the trees. He had no doubt he stood on Sinclair property, and someone had the balls to not just pull a trailer on his grandpa's land but build a house. Blood boiled in his veins, but he couldn't dwell on that now. He needed to solve one problem at a time.

He nodded toward the tattered bungalow with brown siding. "Is this your house?"

Marie emerged from the thick foliage, her footsteps halting so she stood behind him as if she needed his protection from whatever they'd find. Her warmth against his back made his blood heat for a different reason. "Yes."

Her breath tickled his neck, and he swallowed every inappropriate thought her nearness caused. "We need to look inside. Then we need to discuss why you and this guy are living on my grandfather's land."

3

Marie stood in the yard and studied the tattered curtains blocking the windows to the kitchen. She'd grown to despise this house over the last month. She didn't mind the small rooms or the old appliances, it was the memories of abuse that made the bungalow depressing.

The distance from her sister and the isolation in the woods made her skin tingle with anxiety.

"I don't know what you're talking about. Bill rented this place from a buddy," she said, finally answering his question.

She chanced a peek at Nora, and big, green eyes stared back at her. How could such a sweet, good-natured baby come from such a horrible situation? The constant tension and stress-filled atmosphere hadn't affected her sweet nature.

Yet.

Which was why she needed to figure out how to help get Bill thrown in prison. So she could protect her Nora and give her the life she deserved.

The deputy glanced over his shoulder, and his expression stole her breath. The kindness had melted away. Now, in this space, his gaze was hard and cold. Facing forward again, he marched through the knee-high grass.

A sense of defeat engulfed her. Finally, she'd confided in someone, and now his suspicion of her changed his entire demeanor. She'd been a fool. His job was to find a man his grandpa shot, not protect a woman he didn't know. She should have never let shock and fear open her mouth.

A twig snapped behind her, and she bolted for the protection of his tense body, staying no more than a step behind him. Anger radiated from him in waves, shimmering along with the humid air.

Owen stopped short, and she dodged, barely avoiding a collision.

Nora cried out, as if anticipating the being squished between them.

He gripped his moist hands against her biceps, and the smell of his sweat mixed with the coffee still on his breath. The top of her head barely came to his chin, and she lifted her face to meet his gaze. The hard set of his jaw tightened her gut, or maybe it was the way the gentle pressure of his fingertips caused all her nerve endings to combust. Either way, she'd wanted this man to help her, not accuse her of trespassing.

"My grandfather owns miles of land along the river, several north of his house." He nodded toward her house but didn't release his grip. "That puts this structure on his property."

Marie swallowed hard. "There has to be an explanation. How could someone build a house with running water and electricity on someone else's property without their knowledge or consent?" Skirting the law wasn't beyond Bill, but logistics told her Owen had to be wrong.

Owen shrugged, but the grim set of his mouth told her he wasn't convinced of her innocence. "We've got bigger problems right now. I don't see any vehicles. Do you or Bill drive?"

Marie glanced around Owen's broad shoulders. No pickup

sat in its usual spot on the gravel lane. "I don't have a car, but Bill has a red Ford truck. He usually parks it on the side of the house."

"I have to check the house. Since we don't know where Bill is, or could be, you and the baby stay close." Owen reached behind him and retrieved a gun tucked in a holster behind his back.

She tried to keep her gaze away from the shiny metal of the weapon and followed him to the same stoop she'd flown from the night before.

Owen pressed his index finger to his lips, then slowly opened the screen door.

The hinges squeaked, and she cringed, but didn't stop moving until she stepped inside, and the door closed behind her. Cradling Nora close, she gently bounced up and down to keep her content.

"Lock the door and stay in here," Owen said.

She nodded, although he didn't wait to acknowledge her consent before heading into the kitchen. Her gaze stayed glued to his body as he rounded the two-person table then disappeared into the living room.

Holding her breath, she sank to the floor and leaned against the cool surface of the washer. Not even twelve hours had passed since Bill had stumbled home from the bar, and here she was again, scared to death in the stupid laundry room. "We'll leave soon, baby girl. I promise. Then we'll never have to come back here again."

Unbothered, Nora's little mouth widened into a yawn.

A few beats passed. The shifts and groans of the thin floors were the only sounds in the sweltering house. Air conditioning was a luxury they couldn't afford, and the motionless air outside didn't allow a breeze to filter through the rooms. Her heart pounded against her chest, the noises playing with her mind as she tried to make out Owen's footsteps. Sweat collected where Nora's head nestled against her.

A shadow danced across the linoleum floor in the kitchen. She stood and crept onto the balls of her feet. The shadow shifted, and Owen stepped into the muted light. He reholstered his weapon and rubbed the back of his neck, closing his eyes.

Marie rose and kissed Nora's forehead. "Is he here?"

He faced her, eyes now open, and shook his head. "No. But there's something you should see."

Fear licked across her belly. Trepidation slowed her steps as she met Owen in the kitchen. He stood quite a few inches taller than her five-foot, seven-inch frame, but his shoulders drooped and a new weariness weighed him down.

He pressed his fingers to the small of her back, his touch again igniting bits of pleasure up her spine, and led her into the living room. She darted her gaze around the space, but nothing stood out. She raised her chin toward him.

Owen lifted his hand from her back and pointed toward the sofa. "On the floor."

She peered over the cushions.

Blood pooled on the shag carpet, saturating the floor and coating the bottom of the oak coffee table. The metallic scent hung heavy in the hot air. She gripped the hard edge of the sofa to steady herself. "Is that Bill's blood?"

Owen stepped closer and the side of his body brushed against hers. "I don't think so. Anyone who lost that much blood probably died on the spot. It's unlikely Bill would have lost the amount of blood he did back in the woods, found his way home, continued to bleed, then left the house. Doesn't make sense."

Marie pressed the back of her hand to her mouth and fought the nausea swimming in her gut. She leaned against Owen and the side of his body anchored her, keeping her from swaying as emotions assaulted her senses.

"You mentioned Bill bringing another woman home last night. You saw him assault her?"

She closed her eyes and the angry screams and smacks and silence from the night before barreled into her. A strong arm wrapped around her shoulders, pulling her closer. Her nausea intensified. "I heard the smack and a loud thud, like someone falling to the ground."

Pressure built in her chest, making her breaths come out in sharp gasps. She opened her eyes and stared up into Owen's narrowed gaze. Tension tightened his jaw, but the gentle pressure of his hand against her arm told her to trust him. "Do you think he killed her?"

"It's an awfully big coincidence a woman was found dead not far from here, and now we've found a ton of blood in the same place you claim a woman was assaulted. Did you know who she was?"

She shook her head and rubbed a hand over her sternum. "I should have stayed. I might have saved her."

"You would have put yourself and your baby in more danger if you'd stayed. But now you can help by telling us everything you can about Bill. We need to figure out where he'd hide."

"I honestly don't know where he'd go. I'd tell you right now if I did."

He hooked a dark brow. "But you might know where he went last night, where he met this woman. That could help in identifying her, or even lead to friends you don't know about."

"I don't know any of his friends." Embarrassment stained her cheeks. She could only imagine what her relationship with Bill looked like from the outside. She swallowed a snort. As bad as it appeared to Owen, the truth was even worse than he could imagine.

"That's okay. Grab some stuff and let's get you out of here. We'll talk more later. Do you have a place to stay?"

"No." The word croaked from her tight throat and moisture filled her eyes.

A low grumble vibrated from Owen's throat, and he circled his other arm around her, engulfing her in a hug. Warmth spread through her. She melted against him, making sure not to smash the now-sleeping Nora, and pushed away all the voices in her head.

The ones telling her to run, the ones telling her to stay, and the ones telling her that the nightmare she'd been living in for the past month was about to get a whole lot worse.

"There's a women's shelter in the next town over," he said, voice soft and comforting. "It's a nice, comfortable place and they'll keep you and your baby safe."

She cringed. "I don't know. A shelter?"

Depending on anyone but herself made her skin itch. How could she trust people she didn't even know to help her when she couldn't even trust her own mother?

Owen rubbed a slow circle against her back, and her tank top shifted with the motion. "I know the woman who runs the place. She's great, and even has a little one of her own. She'll treat you like family, and even help with the baby while you're there."

"Okay." Marie drew in a deep breath and instantly regretted it as the overpowering stench of blood assaulted her nose. She pulled away and offered Owen a weak smile. She'd go along with his plan for the time being. As much as she hated to admit it, she needed protection right now, and if she could offer any insight into finding her scumbag ex, she would.

Besides, it wasn't like she had anywhere else to go. Her family lived hours away, she didn't have any money, and the man who had invaded her life with a piece of blackmail against her mom was now a possible killer.

He might be injured, and on the run, but that didn't mean she was safe. Bill had lived outside the law and used her mother's addiction to worm his way back into Marie's life. To keep her under his thumb, he'd threatened to throw her mother to the wolves and kill her sister—not to mention what he'd do to Nora. She had no doubt he'd stop at nothing to get her back again.

But this time, she'd do whatever she had to take him down for good.

OWEN MENTALLY CREATED a checklist of all the shit he needed to get done as soon as he got Marie and her little girl settled at Safe Haven Women's Shelter. The drive to Pine Valley was normally one he enjoyed. Winding through the mountains into the quaint little town with so much charm and so many good, solid people.

But not today.

Today he was the lead in a murder investigation, and the beautiful woman beside him was his only witness. A witness with seemingly no answers who was either trapped in a horrible situation or lying.

He'd figure that out later. For now, he had to focus on Marie and Nora. He'd called ahead and spoken with Laura Metcalf, the woman who ran the shelter, and she assured him they'd take good care of Marie and Nora. Not only that, but she'd sent one of the volunteers to Water's Edge with a car seat so he could drive Nora safely in his cruiser.

Sadie Pennel, the volunteer who'd shown up and a fellow Sheriff's Deputy, had offered to take Marie and Nora herself, but Marie's hesitation had him insisting he could play the chauffeur. A quick glance in her direction made him doubt his decision.

"You doing all right?" he asked, peeling his gaze away from her to focus on the road again. She was such an interesting combination of hard and soft. Tough and vulnerable. Instinct told him he needed to keep his distance if at all possible or he'd fall hard for whatever secrets those deep, green eyes held.

She peeked over her shoulder at Nora before facing him. "I don't know. I kind of feel like this isn't my life. That none of this is real. That I didn't get us out of that house alive just to find myself in even more trouble."

He chewed over her words. "Were you in trouble before?"

She dropped her gaze to her clasped hands. The only sound in the car the bubbly gurgles of the baby.

Not wanting to push her too hard, he opted to change the subject. "She seems like a happy baby."

Marie beamed, the first real smile he'd seen since he'd laid eyes on her that morning. "She's the best. Always so happy and sweet. I don't know what I did to deserve such a blessing."

A pinch of sadness squeezed his gut. After the death of his mother when he was younger, he'd spent his life in pursuit of one thing...being an officer of the law. His singular focus had left him with very few relationships and a lot of loneliness. Definitely without hope of a child of his own.

Something he didn't realize he even wanted until recently.

"She looks just like you."

"Thank God for small favors," she said with an indelicate snort. "I don't want her to have anything of her father's."

Her firm tone invited no more comment. He cleared his throat and took the final turn into Pine Valley. The white gazebo in the middle of the grassy square stood out in stark contrast to the blue sky. Red brick lined the sidewalks, and colorful awnings highlighted the mom-and-pop shops clustered along the quiet streets.

Marie sighed.

"You okay?"

She wrinkled her nose as if embarrassed. "Sorry. This town

is just so cute. Like straight out of a storybook. I didn't know places like this actually existed."

Curiosity wedged in his throat. Learning about her personal life might or might not relate to his case, but he had to know for sure before diving into the deep end. He couldn't use his position of authority to pry for his own benefit. "Have you spent any time in downtown Water's Edge?"

Shaking her head, her smile vanished. "Bill liked Nora and me to stay in the house."

"You'd like it. Main Street runs along the river. Lots of local shops and cafes. Seating along the water with great views. A little different than Pine Valley but just as nice."

"Sounds lovely."

More baby babbling sounded from the backseat. He grinned and headed away from town until the three-story Victorian house-turned-shelter appeared. He pulled his cruiser into the driveway and shut off the engine.

"Is this the shelter?" Marie asked, jaw slack.

"Yep. It was a food pantry for years. Mrs. Collins ran it and worked with Laura Metcalf, the woman I'll be introducing you to, to transform it into a shelter."

Marie peered through the window. "Sounds like quite the undertaking. Why did this Laura woman want to create a shelter?"

"That's not my story to tell," he said then pocketed his keys. "If you grab Nora, I'll get the bags you packed."

She blew out a shaky breath and stepped out of the car.

He couldn't react to her nerves. Couldn't suggest an alternate place for her to stay or even keep her with him. He had a job to do, and being around Marie and her quiet beauty would take his focus off the case.

Not to mention it could put her in harm's way.

Heading to the trunk, he hooked the diaper bag and duffle

over his shoulder then waited for Marie to detach the car seat from the base hooked in his backseat.

"Hey, y'all. Welcome." Laura stood on the porch and waved. Her long blond hair was tied in a messy knot at the top of her head. She kept her smile in place as she walked down the steps of the wide porch and stopped in front of Marie. "You must be Marie, and who is this beautiful little princess?"

"This is Nora."

"Two? Three months?"

"Two," Marie said.

"Girl, we've got a lot to talk about. My little one is nine months old. She's the light of my life and such a little stinker. No one understands motherhood like another mother. But let's get you two up to your room first."

Laura led the way into the house, waiting for them all to get inside the large foyer before speaking again. "I have a room set up for you on the second floor. Owen, you can leave the bags here. I'll help Marie take them upstairs."

Owen set the bags on the floor then faced Marie. She was in good hands, but the uncertainty in her eyes twisted his gut. "I'll be in touch, okay?"

She nodded.

He rubbed the back of his neck, searching for anything else to say to postpone his departure. "Is there anything else I can do for you before I leave?"

Laura scooped up the discarded bags. "I've got them, Owen."

He gave the baby snuggled in her seat one more long glance before locking eyes with Marie. The bruise circling her eye made his blood boil and reminded him he had a job to do.

He needed to find the bastard who'd hit her—and possibly murdered another woman—then Marie could really get on with her life.

Far away from him.

4

The mattress dipped under Marie's weight as she settled on the pretty bed in her temporary room. Gratitude and fear battled against each other, setting her nerves on edge. She'd never lived in such a beautiful space before. With the four-poster bed and cream eyelet comforter. A fuzzy rug covered the wooden floors, and a tall dresser was tucked in the corner. There was even a rocking chair where she could feed Nora once she woke.

And the air conditioning.

Closing her eyes, she sighed and enjoyed the cool blast of air that flowed down from vents in the textured ceiling. If she wasn't terrified Bill would find her and make her pay for leaving, she could stay here forever.

A soft knock at the door opened her eyes.

"Do you need anything?" Laura stood in the doorway. Something about the way she kept her distance, didn't push or intrude, told Marie this woman held a world of stories inside her.

Stories similar to the ones Marie had lived.

Marie looked around the room, still surprised to find herself there. "No, thanks."

"Do you mind if I come in?" Laura asked.

"Sure." Marie braced herself for whatever was to come. She didn't have many friends, and she didn't have a playbook on how to have a conversation with a stranger offering her and her baby a safe place to stay. Her walls were high, no matter how friendly Laura had been.

Laura stopped to stare down at Nora, asleep in the portable crib beside the bed before lowering herself onto the rocking chair. "Seems like just yesterday Isla was that tiny. Time goes by so fast. Now she's crawling all over the place. Saying real words. It's crazy."

"Is she here?" Marie asked.

"My mom has her in the play area we have set up for the children who stay here. We try to always have someone on hand in case mothers need a little break or have somewhere to be. We never seem to be low on volunteers to hold a baby or watch the children."

Marie stared down at Nora's pouty lips and full cheeks. "I can't imagine letting anyone else take care of her. I haven't spent one second away from her since she was born."

"People say it takes a village, but some people don't understand that's not always an option. No one here will make you leave that precious baby's side if you don't want to, but the service is there if you'd like to use it. We also have group meetings. Some with therapists, some led by women who've been in similar situations."

Marie snorted. "I don't think anyone has ever found themselves in a situation like mine."

A hint of sadness crept into Laura's eyes for a quick second. "Everyone who comes through these doors has their own hardships—their own burdens. We do what we can to help."

"I really appreciate you letting me stay here while everything gets figured out. I'm not sure how much Deputy Wells told you, but I didn't have anywhere else to go. And if my ex finds me..."

Tears welled in her eyes. She dashed them away, unwilling to shed any tears for a man she couldn't stand.

Laura moved to sit beside her and took her hand, squeezing gently. "He told me enough to know we need to keep our guard up—something we have experience with. The women who run this shelter are survivors. We're strong. And we're here for one another. We protect each other, so don't worry. Okay?"

Marie drew in a shuddering breath, wishing she could believe what this sweet, young woman told her.

"But in the meantime, let me know if you need anything at all. There are diapers and wipes in the dresser, and I found some extra clothes for the baby. There are more in the room downstairs where we keep donations. Feel free to take whatever you need. Lunch is at noon."

"Should I help or just stay in my room?" She felt ridiculous asking, but she didn't know what was expected.

Laura patted her hand then stood. "You can help Mrs. Collins—the owner of the house—cook or come down when it's finished. But there are no rules about how you spend your time. You're not a prisoner here, you're a guest. I just recommend letting someone know if you leave, and honestly, you probably shouldn't go anywhere alone. Would you like my phone number? Then you can call me at any time."

Heat scorched her cheeks. "I don't have a phone."

"Then let's go get you one. We always have prepaid phones on hand for guests to use. I can give you a tour of the house while we're at it. Then you can see everything we offer."

"Sounds good," Marie said, happy to have a plan.

"Can I carry the baby for you?" Laura asked.

A slight hesitation slowed Marie's response. She didn't trust anyone with her baby, but it was time she started. Standing, she scooped up Nora and handed her over to Laura. She followed the other woman out of the room and a tiny bit of the burden she'd carried on her shoulders since leaving her family slipped away. She'd only had herself to depend on for so damn long. It was time to move forward and get on with her life.

But first, she had to make sure she and Nora wouldn't just be safe for the next few days, but forever.

OWEN SAT in his car and soaked up another second of the cool air blasting from the vents before heading back inside the shack Marie had suffered in over the past month. He still needed to ask his grandpa about the house on the old man's property, but he had more important things to focus on.

He'd deal with the trespassing issue later.

First, he needed to identify the woman in the river and find the man his gut told him was responsible for her death.

Movement in the rearview mirror caught his attention and the muscles in the pit of his stomach knotted. A sheriff's cruiser bounded down the lane, and one glance at the broad form with the wide-brim hat behind the wheel told Owen who drove toward him. He would have contacted his dad at some point to fill him in on the pile of crap his grandpa had stepped into, but he'd hoped to have some more answers before they spoke.

Relishing one more blast of cold air, Owen shut off his car and swung the door open to the heat box outside. His phone vibrated against his leg, and he checked the screen as he stood tall and waited for his dad to park.

Dad's on his way. Sorry. I'll be there in ten.

Owen snorted and shoved the phone back in his pocket. So much for a heads up, but at least Tommy tried to warn him.

A car door slammed shut and birds scattered into the blue

sky. Sheriff Mike Wells marched his way, his hard gaze taking in everything around them.

Owen would have to make sure to keep a tight lid on his attraction to Marie, or his dad would have a thing or two to say about that.

"One dead body and another blood-filled crime scene, and you didn't think to call me?" Mike halted his abrupt pace in front of Owen, blocking his view of the house, and a cloud of dust swam around their ankles.

Owen clasped his hands in front of him and fought the urge to shuffle his feet—or worse, roll his eyes. He'd been a deputy long enough that he didn't feel the need to call his dad every time trouble came to town. "I've been a bit busy. I'd have called when I had more to tell you."

Mike nodded toward the house. "How'd you find this place, and why did you enter without a warrant?"

"Did you seriously come all the way out here to ask me if I broke protocol by entering a house without cause?"

"No, I came to see if you need help. Crimes like this don't come along every day. I can be more helpful than Tommy. You shouldn't have him in on this. He's too green."

A heavy hand came down on Owen's shoulder, and he tensed under the pressure. He tried to gauge his father's sincerity—his calm, monotone voice never belied the man's emotions—but the shadows cast by Mike's hat hid the facial features so much like his own. "We need every man we can get on this, and Tommy was first on scene. You know as well as I do the first officer to take in a crime scene counts for a lot."

Mike sighed and dropped his hand to his side then turned to face the house. "I don't like having two of my sons so close to a murder investigation."

The twinge of fatigue in his dad's voice was like a punch in the gut. A grisly crime scene from years ago still haunted their family, always lingering in the back of their minds.

Except for Pappy. The unsolved hit-and-run murder of his only daughter—Owen's mother—lived in the forefront of his mind and dictated every decision he made.

And the guilt his father harbored led to him trying to control the choices of his children. Owen had been old enough to stand up to his father's constant interference, but his brother and sister had a more difficult time.

Owen stepped beside his dad and followed his line of sight to the bungalow, knowing full well the dilapidated house tucked away in the woods wasn't what weighed Mike down. "You can't protect us. We made our choices."

"I know." Mike nodded and faced forward. "Tell me about this place. The crime scene unit will be here shortly. Let's head inside and take a look until they get here."

Owen led the way and mentally prepared for the conversation, securing a pair of gloves while he spoke. He launched into his encounter as he mounted the porch steps and crossed the threshold into Marie's house, nodding to the officer he'd placed outside the front door to protect the scene.

Mike grumbled and huffed along with the story then let out a low whistle when the pool of blood became visible. "Sounds like Lewis got himself involved in a fine mess and dragged you along with him." He squatted and studied the blood splattered around the living room.

Owen bristled. "He didn't drag me into anything. This woman needed help, and she's lucky he was around."

Mike stood. "Where's the girl now?"

"She's staying at the women's shelter over in Pine Valley. She's not from here and had no place to go. I've got every available set of eyes in the department looking for her boyfriend and nothing so far. If he knows where she is, I think he might go after her." Owen walked the perimeter of the room, keeping his eyes peeled for anything he'd missed earlier.

"Did she take a purse?"

Owen glanced at his dad with raised brows. "Excuse me?"

"Women always take a purse, but there's a big bag tucked behind the television stand."

Owen rounded the couch and glanced in the direction of the television. Sure enough, a large bag laid sprawled on its side. Curiosity moved him forward. He yanked on the brown strap and freed the bag from its hiding space. The force sent lipstick, business cards, and a wallet sprawling to the shag carpet.

Grabbing the wallet, he flipped it open and pulled out the first credit card he found. "This isn't Marie's bag. Credit card belongs to an Erica Zyler." Adrenaline zipped through his veins, and he thumbed through the rest of the cards until he found a driver's license. The picture boasted a petite woman with blue eyes and dark blonde hair. A healthy glow darkened her skin instead of the pale, bloated face he'd seen floating in the river this morning, but there was no denying the resemblance. "This is the woman who was found this morning. We need to get someone to notify her next of kin."

A sliver of plastic poked out from beneath the stand, and Owen bent to grab it. He studied the name—same name as the credit card and license—and read the title beside the picture.

Shock vibrated his core and he stood, facing his dad with the ID badge crushed in his fist. "Erica wasn't just some chick Bill brought home from the bar. She was a reporter."

5

Exhaustion tightened the muscles in Marie's neck. She fought to relax as Nora struggled to nurse. Usually Nora was an eating champ, but there was no way her baby hadn't picked up on the stress chipping away at Marie. No matter how hard she tried to stay calm and serene for Nora's benefit—something she'd had to do since her daughter's birth—today's development was too much.

Too upsetting.

Too dangerous.

Bill might be an asshole, but Marie had known him most of her life. She could read his moods and guess what he'd do before he'd even made the decision. But now he was out there. Pissed, hurt, and in more trouble than she'd imagined.

And he'd want to get his hands on her no matter the price.

Nora's frustrated cries snapped her back to the moment. Fat tears slid down her red face.

"I'm sorry, baby girl. Let's take a little break. I think we both need it." Marie readjusted her shirt and stood with Nora in her arms. She pressed her lips to Nora's forehead, bouncing up and down to calm her. "See, we're okay, girlie. You and me against the world, right? Mommy loves you so much. I'll make sure you're always safe. No matter what."

Nora's happy gurgles made her smile.

Savory scents wafted through the cracks under the door, reminding her that Nora wasn't the only one who hadn't eaten much today.

"How about we venture downstairs and see what's for lunch? No reason to stay in here all day."

Tying the homemade wrap around her chest, she nestled Nora inside and made her way downstairs. She couldn't help but run her fingers along the gleaming woodwork on the banister or poke her head into one of the sitting rooms on the first floor. Laura had given her a brief tour of the second and third floors, but there was still so much left to discover. She could lose herself for hours in this house.

A swinging door that led to the back of the house opened and an older woman with gray hair, glasses, and bright smile burst into the foyer. "Perfect timing, my dear. I was just about to let you know lunch is ready if you're hungry. I'm Mrs. Collins, by the way." She wiped her palm on the white-and-blue checked apron tied around her waist then offered it to Marie.

Marie secured Nora with one palm and shook Mrs. Collins' hand with the other. "Hello."

The door swung open again and a little girl bounded out on her tiptoes. Brown hair was tied in pigtails with little red ribbons. "I'm starving," she said, with enough drama to make Marie believe she hadn't eaten in days. "Can we eat now?"

Mrs. Collins clicked her tongue. "Amelia, don't be rude. This is our new guest, and we need to make sure she's fed too."

Amelia's little mouth made a small o shape before grinning. "You have a baby! I love babies. Can I hold her?"

Hesitation stole Marie's words. This child couldn't be more than five or six years old. No way she could let her hold Nora, but she didn't want to offend anyone.

Mrs. Collins pulled the small child to her side. "Give her space, love. Let's sit and eat some lunch, get to know her a little before we start trying to hold the baby. Deal?"

Amelia swished her lips to the side and stared up at Mrs. Collins, as if giving her suggestion serious consideration. "Deal. Mom's getting out plates. Let's go!" She turned and ran back the way she'd come without waiting for an answer.

Mrs. Collins chuckled. "She comes with her mom to volunteer. A very rambunctious child with lots of personality."

"She reminds me of my sister," Marie said, smiling. "She's a teenager now, but there's enough of an age gap that I still remember when she was that age. Always smiling and full of life."

"Are you still close?"

A familiar pang of longing forced her to tighten her smile. She wanted nothing more than to return home and be with her sister, but Bill had taken that option away. "As close as we can be."

Mrs. Collins offered her a sympathetic look, setting her emotions into overdrive. Tears threatened to swell in her eyes, and she sniffed them back. Kindness and compassion weren't things she'd been on the receiving end of recently. She'd forgotten how nice it was to have people around who cared about her.

"Come now," Mrs. Collins said, anchoring a forearm against the small of Marie's back and leading her through the swinging door and into the kitchen.

A colorful explosion of flowers in clear vases sat in the middle of a large, farmhouse table at the far end of the room and on the giant island. White marble set off the light gray of the cabinets and soft blue mosaic tiles covered the wall above the countertops.

Amelia knelt on a high stool tucked under the lip of the island. She grabbed a slice of toasted bread from a stack and lined it with bacon from a plate beside her. She glanced over her shoulder before returning her focus to assembling her lunch. "See, Mama. A baby."

The woman who'd brought the car seat for Nora stood on the other side of the island and sliced a red tomato. The freckles across her face mirrored that of her daughter's, as did her emerald green eyes. "I know, honey. I met them both earlier." She offered Marie a small smile. "I'm Sadie."

"I remember," Marie said. "Thank you again for the car seat. You were a life saver."

She waved away the compliment. "It's what I'm here for. Amelia and I like to volunteer whenever we have time, or until Mrs. Collins kicks us out. Sometimes we can overstay our welcome a bit." She widened her eyes then winked at Amelia.

Amelia giggled. "Mrs. Collins lobes me."

The way the little girl pronounced the v in love melted Marie's heart. "How could she not?"

Amelia grinned. "Wanna samwich?"

"Or she can make her own," Sadie said, then slid the sliced tomatoes in her direction. "Take a seat. You're our only guest right now so no need to wait for anyone else. Would you like me to hold the little one for you so you have two free hands?"

Mrs. Collins cleared her throat. "Excuse me, but I call dibs. If and when she's ready to hand her over. Go ahead and sit."

Marie pinged her attention around the room, trying to keep up with all the banter. Being trapped for so long with only Nora and Bill for company had left her social skills rusty.

Not to mention her nerves were stretched so tight, she had a hard time keeping her mind on anything other than the mess that led her here.

But if she wanted to ever make a better life for her and Nora, she needed to put Bill and all his abuse and his scheming and his bullshit in her rearview mirror. She needed to figure out her new normal without him. She had to trust these women—and one very cute girl—to help her.

She summoned all the courage Bill had tried to stomp out of her and plucked Nora from her carrier. "I haven't had two hands to eat in a very long time. Sounds wonderful." She handed her most precious gift to Mrs. Collins then took a seat beside Amelia, who gleefully made her a sandwich.

This was the beginning of her new life, even if Bill still loomed large, and her first step toward freedom. She took a big bite and grinned. "This is the most delicious thing I've ever eaten."

Owen rummaged through the rest of the bag, hoping to find more information about the woman who'd owned the purse. Bill had to be nuts if he thought no one would notice his poor excuse of a hiding place where he'd stuffed Erica's personal items, but he probably didn't count on being shot by a crazy old man before he could clean up his mess.

A light tap sounded on the front door before it swung open.

Tommy entered the room, and his eyes widened. An unnatural paleness swept over his bronze face. Sandy blond hair brushed across his forehead, moisture clumping together the longer-than-usual strands. He cleared his throat, tore his gaze from the blood, and locked eyes with first Mike, then Owen. "The crime scene unit is here."

Owen returned the purse to the floor and stood. "Okay. Let's step outside and talk."

His dad followed him to the door, and Owen led the way back to his car. He nodded his greeting to the individuals who'd arrived to go over the house with a fine-tooth comb. "We need to find the bastard who lives here."

Tommy glanced around. "Isn't this Pappy's property?"

Owen's gaze flickered to his dad for a beat then focused on Tommy again. His coloring had returned to normal, and he'd hidden his hazel eyes behind a pair of aviator sunglasses. "I thought the same thing. I want to ask him about it, but why don't you do some digging? See whose name is on the deed. The woman who lives here claims they rented the house from a friend. If she's lying—or more likely in the dark about what's going on—we need to find out who got a house with running water and electricity on Pappy's land without him knowing."

Tommy pressed his lips together, squaring his strong jaw and showing his displeasure. "Do you really think that's the best way to use me right now? A woman is dead and the suspect is at large. Let me help find him."

"Tommy." Mike drew out his name the same way he'd done when Tommy had been in trouble as a boy. He shifted his weight and pulled up his pants, even though they sat snuggly around his expanding middle.

Owen held up a hand. "You don't need to interfere, Dad." He brought his attention back to his brother. "Someone rented out this house, and finding out who could be a big part in finding Bill. We don't know much about this guy, but the woman who lives here mentioned him not having many friends. They're new to town. The owner of this house may be the only connection."

"I didn't think about that," Tommy said.

"That's why you're the rookie." Owen lightened his tone and smirked. He wanted Tommy to help with the investigation, but he always wanted him to know his place. "Dad, you want a job?"

Mike snorted out a laugh, and the shadows from his hat couldn't hide the wrinkles around his pale blue eyes. "I'm the sheriff. I don't need you assigning me a job."

Owen narrowed his eyes and quirked a brow. "Really? When's the last time you got out from behind that big desk of yours? You're an elected official now, not a uniform patrolling the streets."

"Doesn't mean I forgot how. But you're right, it's been a while, and you're the lead on this. I can take orders as well as anyone." Mike tipped the brim of his hat and showed the tiny lift of his lips. "When I have to."

Despite the pressure suffocating Owen to do his job, he laughed. "Call the paper where Erica Zyler worked. Find out if it's just a coincidence this woman was at the bar with Bill Flanders, or if it's something deeper."

Mike frowned. "You think she was investigating him?"

Owen shrugged. "Makes sense to me. Why else murder a random woman you brought home from the bar? He has a history of abusive behavior, but nothing to indicate he's gone this far before."

"How do you know this guy's history?" Tommy asked, taking a step forward.

"The woman who lives with him was at Pappy's this morning. She ran last night, the guy followed her through the woods, and Pappy shot him."

Tommy whistled and rubbed a palm over his smooth baby face. "Dang. Things keep getting messier."

A mosquito landed on Owen's forearm and the tiny pinch of its bite pieced his skin. He swatted it and grabbed his car keys from his pocket. "We all know what we need to do."

Mike hesitated and darted his gaze from Owen to Tommy and back again. "You want Tommy working alone on this?"

Tension filled the heated air. Their sheriff's department was too small for Owen to have the luxury of a partner but sending Tommy out on his own caused apprehension to squeeze his gut. He didn't want to micromanage Tommy, but partnering the boy up with someone with experience would be beneficial—it would keep Owen from worrying about his brother and help his brother learn.

"I'm not a child." Tommy ground out the words through clenched teeth.

"You don't want to work with me on this?" Owen tilted his head to the side and studied his brother as an idea formed.

An idea he had no doubt Tommy would hate.

Tommy ran a hand through his sandy blonde hair, sending the strands to stick straight into the air. "I didn't say that. I just mean I don't need my big brother looking after me. I know how to do my job."

"No one's saying you don't," Mike said. "But this is a big case and the first one you've worked. Having someone with a little more experience could benefit you."

Tommy opened his mouth, but Owen jumped in before he could get out any words. "I agree. I'd tell you to come with me, but we each have our own line to tug, and I can't waste time checking in. I think you and Dad should team up. Ride together, bounce ideas off each other, and keep me posted if anything comes up."

Red stained Tommy's cheeks, and he fisted his hands at his sides.

If the situation wasn't so serious, Owen would laugh at how many times the boy's coloring could change in five minutes.

"I don't need a babysitter."

"Not saying you do. But you could use the help." Owen locked gazes with Tommy, then Mike, before he continued. "And I don't need to waste any more time discussing this."

"Where are you going?" Mike adjusted his hat and pulled his keys from his front pocket.

"Safe Haven Women's Shelter. I need to talk to Marie. I need to find out everything I can about this guy, and she's the only link we have. If you two discover anything useful, call me."

Mike nodded and Tommy grunted, then followed their dad toward his cruiser.

Owen watched them go. He'd either made a brilliant move

by putting them together, or they'd kill each other before nightfall.

Opening his car door, he sat on the scorching leather and started the engine. Air poured from the vents, and even though it wasn't cold yet, the artificial gust of wind was far better than the heat outside. Anticipation zipped through him as he maneuvered out of the lane. He needed to speak with Marie. She may have the answers he needed to catch a killer.

An image of her full lips and wide green eyes flashed in his brain, and his groin tightened. He didn't doubt she was in trouble, but he couldn't help but wonder how she'd found herself in such a desperate situation—twice. She didn't fit the profile of most abused women he came across. Marie had secrets, and he planned on uncovering all of them.

6

Butterflies danced in the pit of Marie's stomach, keeping rhythm with the ticking of the clock in the sitting room. Lunch in the pretty kitchen with the friendly company had been nice and not nearly long enough, cut short by a call from Deputy Wells. He needed to speak with her and was on his way to do so in person.

She pressed a hand to her belly, willing the frantically flapping wings to stop before she threw up. Speaking with the handsome deputy was her only way to help find Bill. The only way to help get justice for a young woman who was killed and tossed in the river like yesterday's trash.

The pool of blood from her living room invaded her mind's eye. Her gut told her Bill knew she witnessed him kill the woman he'd brought home last night. Would he still come after her if the police were after him?

Absolutely.

It would be reckless and stupid, but he wouldn't just let her walk away. Especially if he thought she saw what he'd done. He'd drag her down with him or die trying. And if he escaped, then he'd go after her family.

A soft knock echoed from the front of the house, followed by murmuring voices and the opening and closing of a door and the sound of footsteps on old wood. Anxiety ricocheted through her.

Owen peeked around the doorframe and lifted a hand in greeting.

Laura stood beside him.

She tried to smile, but it wobbled on her lips.

"Do you two want to talk in here?" Laura asked. "Or I can make a fresh pot of coffee."

"Either's fine, but I'd love some coffee," Owen said and lingered in the doorway.

"We can head into the kitchen. No reason to bring everything in here." Marie stood and clasped her hands in front of her waist. "Is Nora okay?"

Beaming, Laura nodded. "Her and Isla are already best friends, and Amelia is loving keeping them both entertained. Would you like me to bring her down?"

A part of her wanted to say yes. Not having Nora with her was like missing a limb. But she'd rather shield her from the heavy and stressful conversation to come, even if she was too young to understand. "As long as she's fine upstairs with you and your mom, let them have fun."

"Holler if you change your mind, and Owen, you know how to work the machine. Grab whatever you need."

Marie followed Owen into the kitchen and sat on the tufted chair situated around the table. She loved this room. The dark wood of the floor and brass knobs on the cabinets gave the space warmth while still being modern. Light flooded in from the window above the porcelain sink. The salty scent of bacon hung heavy in the air from the BLTs she'd shared with new friends.

Owen moved through the kitchen, grabbing what he needed. As the machine chugged to life, he faced her. Dark circles hung under his eyes. "I've got every deputy in the county looking for Bill. No one has seen him or his truck."

Unease burrowed into her chest and she rubbed her collarbone, hoping to relieve some of the pressure.

"Do you know a woman named Erica Zyler?"

She crinkled her forehead and tried to recall the name. A few people ventured into their crappy rental, but no one she'd spoken with. She'd preferred to stay out of sight and out of mind. People tended to speak more freely when observers weren't around, and she needed to gather as much evidence against Bill as possible to free herself from the chains binding her to him. "The name doesn't ring a bell."

Owen turned back to the now silent coffee machine, filled two mugs, and settled across from her at the table. "We believe she's the woman Bill brought back to your house last night, and the woman who was found dead this morning."

A shudder ripped through her. She covered her mouth with her hand and prayed she wouldn't be sick. "I shouldn't have left her. I should have done more to help her." Emotion tightened her throat and tears rimmed her eyes.

"You can't blame yourself. Because of you, now we know who she is. But we need to figure out why your boyfriend would kill her. You mentioned he's hit you. Does he have other violent tendencies you're aware of?"

She lowered her hand to her throat and cleared away the tears. "He's not my boyfriend. Our relationship is...complicated."

Owen nodded, but curiosity clouded his eyes, making the green overshadow the brown.

Ignoring his unasked question, she focused on answering the one he'd verbalized. "Like I said before, Bill has a temper when he's drunk. He gets off on smacking women around, proving how powerful he is." She rolled her eyes and snorted. "Power—and control—are very important to him."

"How so?" Owen leaned forward and kept his gaze locked on her, his steaming coffee untouched in front of him.

Marie took a deep breath. Best to dive in from the beginning. "I've known Bill most my life. Everyone knows everyone in the town we grew up in."

Owen grunted and settled back in his seat, grabbing his coffee. "Sounds like Water's Edge."

Marie smiled. Water's Edge did remind her of home. "Bill didn't come from a good home. His father abused him, and he spent most of his adolescent years trying to prove he was stronger, smarter than the dad who abandoned him."

Owen bobbed his head as he sipped his coffee but didn't interrupt.

"My dad took off when I was little, so I understood him. That bonded us in a way and brought us together. We dated all through high school." She dropped her gaze and stared into the dark liquid in the white ceramic mug Owen had set on the table. Her nerves were on edge enough without adding caffeine.

Owen raised one brow and returned his mug to the table. "What happened? If you two haven't dated in years, why move with him to a town where you don't know anyone?"

A war waged inside her, and she debated how much to tell him. She wanted him to understand why she was with a man like Bill, but as stupid as it sounded, she didn't want him to think less of her by exposing all the horrors of her past.

She weighed her words carefully. "My mom found herself in some trouble, and Bill was the only person who could get her out of it. His only stipulation was I had to agree to leave town with him. As soon as I agreed, he took me away from my friends and family. He's kept me as isolated as possible—especially once Nora was in the picture. No jobs, no friends...I don't even have a phone to stay connected with anyone."

Owen narrowed his gaze and worked his jaw back and

forth. "What kind of trouble was your mom in? What could make you leave your home?"

Sucking in a deep breath, she summoned her courage. She needed to lay all her cards on the table. "My mom is a drug addict. Has been for as long as I can remember. She was put on probation last year and things got better, but then Bill showed me a video of her selling drugs. If he turns in the video, she'd go to jail for a long time."

She barreled on before she lost her nerve. "I had to save my mom and protect my sister. I just needed to bide my time until I could dig up enough dirt on Bill. If I leave him, he'll go back for my family. He'll try to take Nora from me. He's threatened to do horrible things, and I can't let that happen. But if I can make him pay, if I can find a way to get him behind bars where he can't hurt anyone else, then Nora and I can walk away."

A weight lifted from her shoulders, but she struggled to breathe as she waited for his response. She dropped her gaze, unable to look into those eyes staring at her—eyes with tiny specks of yellow sprinkled throughout the mossy green.

Eyes that devoured every word, every motion, every damn thought in her head. A shiver danced down her spine. If his eyes devoured her, what would the rest of him do?

His ringing phone snapped her from her inappropriate thoughts.

He offered an apologetic smile then answered. "Hi, Pappy. What's up?"

Owen frowned and Marie caught crumbles of Lewis' irritated voice.

"Okay. I'll stop by the house. Hold on a second." He cupped his palm over the speaker. "I hate to ask you to do this. Pappy still has the tapes I need to see, and it'd be helpful if you could identify Bill on the footage. Would you mind coming with me?"

Anticipation zipped down her spine and she nodded.

Finally, she might get to play a hand in putting Bill where he belonged and spend more time with Owen in the process.

She mentally groaned. She was a single mother with no job, no money, and a world of baggage. Spending time with any man was the last thing she should be thinking about—no matter how handsome he was.

Because when it came to hunky men who were out of her league, Deputy Owen Wells took the cake. Forgetting that would be a huge mistake.

OWEN TAPPED LIGHTLY on his grandfather's door before opening it wide for Marie to step inside. He followed behind and a wall of heat greeted him. "The old man needs to invest in some air conditioning."

"I'm used to the heat." Marie shot him a tentative smile and crossed her arms over her chest.

He studied her furrowed brow and the unease in her round eyes. "You okay?"

"Not really." She shrugged and set her purse on the floor and slipped off her shoes. "I've never been away from Nora before. Leaving her with people I barely know feels irresponsible, but I didn't want her to be around all this negative energy. It's hard to know what's the right decision sometimes."

He resisted cringing at her inner turmoil over her child. He didn't have the extra burden of constantly thinking about someone else's needs. Being a mother had to be exhausting, especially with no support. "I understand that, but trust me, she's in the safest hands possible. Laura will call if anything happens, and the second you want to go back to the shelter, I'll take you."

"Thank you."

Lewis appeared and cleared his throat. His plaid shirt was

wrinkled and old jeans practically fell from his slim frame. "I told you to leave her alone."

Owen bit back a sigh. "I can't do that."

He glanced at Marie. She stood wide-eyed with a whisper of a smile on her full lips. Her long, raven black hair tumbled around her shoulders, and not a stitch of make-up covered her skin. His stomach knotted. She was knee-deep in trouble, and he needed her help. But he hated to admit there was something else pulling him to her, a magnetic force drawing him to her side and demanding he discover everything about her.

Blinking, he tore his gaze away from her. He couldn't get caught up in some insane attraction, couldn't get caught up in the weird emotions that stirred in his gut whenever he even thought about her little girl. He had a job to do, nothing more.

"Lewis, I want to help." Marie spoke with an authority that contradicted the fatigue etched on the fine lines of her face.

Lewis shook his head. "Getting involved with something you aren't trained to deal with can be dangerous. You need to stay away, girl."

"But this situation involves me. No one around here knows Bill, and if I can help find him, I will. What he did to that poor woman makes me sick. He deserves to go to prison. That's the only way Nora and I will be free."

A tiny shudder shook her shoulders, and Owen balled his hands into fists to keep from reaching out to her.

"Fine." The word passed through Lewis' mouth with a small grunt. "Let's go look at those tapes. I queued them up."

"You sure you're up to this?" Owen asked, even though he'd been the one to request she view the tapes.

She stiffened her shoulders and lifted her chin, showing off her long neck. "Yes."

Her flash of feistiness brought a smile to his lips, and he nodded.

Dread slowed his steps as he approached Pappy's bedroom.

He hated stepping into this space—hated his mother's haunted eyes starting at him from the walls. Marie would have a lot of questions after witnessing Lewis' cave. He hoped she'd keep them to herself, at least until they were out of his grandpa's range of hearing. One reason he kept his distance these days was because he couldn't endure more talk about his long-gone mother or his grandpa's quest to find her killer.

Lewis flipped on a light and settled into a brown leather desk chair in front of a large computer monitor.

Pictures of his mother littered the walls, and he averted his gaze from the wall-to-wall papers plastered around the room. He didn't have to look at the corkboard above the bed to know photos of suspects hung like posters of the pinup models he'd had in his room as a teenager. He didn't have to glance in the corner to know files and notes cluttered the bookcase, a constant reminder of the unsolved case his grandpa would never turn his back on.

A hit-and-run accident that had taken his mother's life and left a world of pain in its wake.

Owen focused all his attention toward the large desk in front of the lone window in the room. Two smaller televisions flanked the screen, all three turned to grainy images of the woods.

"I started these at different times, all after I shot that sonofabitch and came inside. If you want to watch that, I can find it next. But I think you'll be more interested in this."

"Have you watched it?"

Owen leaned forward, not wanting to miss anything. Marie pressed in beside him, and the scent of coconuts wafted up his nose. He wanted to bend down and bury his nose in her silky strands. He gritted his teeth to keep his attention on what his grandpa had to show him.

Lewis lifted a bony finger and pointed at the corner of the middle screen. "The time stamp shows this was about an hour after I came inside. This camera is pointed at the edge of my property, so you won't see much. But it's enough."

Owen raised a brow. "Enough for what?"

Lewis said nothing, just clicked his tongue and kept his finger extended toward the computer.

A flutter of branches caught Owen's attention on the top of the screen, and his gaze followed Lewis' finger as it trailed down to a shadow. He squinted, trying to morph the movements into concrete shapes. "What am I looking at?"

A hand tightened on his arm. "Feet."

He glanced at Marie and took note of her pale cheeks then quickly turned back to the surveillance footage. The outline of two feet took form. "It's the bottoms of the feet."

Lewis nodded. "Give it a second."

As if on command another shadow emerged on the edge of the screen. The figure moved quickly, pushing leaves and branches out of the way.

Owen's narrowed gaze followed the silhouette of what he assumed was Bill, an arm looped around dainty ankles, moving through the forest. The man stumbled a few times and grabbed his side, then righted himself and continued down the hill. Owen's blood boiled. Not only had he killed a woman, but he'd dragged her down the riverbank like she was nothing more than a prize buck taken down during deer season.

"Is that another shadow?" Marie whispered the question into the quiet room, the soft sound of her words competing with the low buzz of the old-as-dirt computer tower buzzing at their feet.

Owen held his breath and watched the third shadow take form. As the first silhouette dragged the ankles further from the camera, another figure lifted two arms above the woman's head. The two hulking figures maneuvered through the brush until they disappeared from view, replaced with the serene landscape that gave no indication of being disturbed by monsters.

Lewis stopped the video. "I fast forwarded the footage and there's no more images of the two men. They must have gone back up the bank further down the river, closer to their property."

"I was there today, and I could have sworn their house was on your property, Pappy. I'm surprised you don't have a camera closer to their house."

Lewis shrugged. "I sold some land a few years back."

Questions burned the back of Owen's tongue, but he swallowed them and focused on Marie instead. "Was one of those men Bill?"

Marie bit the plumpy flesh of her bottom lip, and her chin trembled. "Yes."

Owen nodded. "No shock there. But you said he didn't have any friends here. Obviously he's close enough to someone that they'd help him dump a dead body."

"He's had a few people at the house. I wrote down any names I heard, but most of the time it was only the first name or nicknames used."

Lewis swiveled in his seat. "You kept records of people coming into your house?"

Owen fought not to roll his eyes at the approval shining from his grandpa's gaze. Only Pappy would have admiration in his voice over recording people's whereabouts in their own home. "Do you remember any of these names?"

Marie straightened and a subtle curve lifted the side of her mouth. "Most of them, but I have the notes in my purse. I'll show you everything."

Finally, something was going his way. Water's Edge was a small town, and if he could connect one of the names in Marie's notes with a resident of the town, he'd be one step closer to finding Bill.

Best yet, if he could get the name of who his grandpa sold the piece of property to that Bill and Marie lived on. Someone had to have the deed, and that someone had to know Bill to rent out that shack.

A vibration pulsed against his thigh, and he grabbed his phone from his pocket and waited for Marie to leave the room before answering the call. "What do you got, Tommy?"

"We found Bill's truck." A beat of silence pulsed through the phone before Tommy said, "He's not with the vehicle. It was abandoned outside of town."

Muttered curses flew from Owen's mouth. Luck be damned, he'd find this guy one way or the other. "Where? I'm on my way."

7

Marie scooped her bag from the worn wooden floor in the living room and plopped it on the upholstered sofa. Rummaging through the bag, she searched for the tattered notebook where she logged all her information regarding Bill.

The police wouldn't need it to tie him to a crime—he'd done a good enough job of that himself—but there could be something she'd seen or heard that could lead them to where the weasel was hiding.

Grabbing the worn book, she hurried across the hall as Owen rushed through the doorway.

A scowl drew down the corners of his mouth, and he rubbed the back of his tanned neck. The motion caused the muscles of his bicep to strain against the gray T-shirt with the Sheriff's Department logo above his right pec. His mud-splattered shirt and faded jeans fit him to perfection, but an image of him in a uniform formed in her mind, and she swallowed hard.

Flustered, she thrust the book forward. "Here's the notebook."

Owen slid his hand from around his neck and grabbed the notebook, his fingers brushing against hers. Heat scorched her cheeks. She yanked back her hand and rocked on her heels, gazing past him into Lewis' room.

"Thanks," Owen said. He flipped through the pages then rounded the binding into his palm. "I need to go. I'll look at this when I get a chance."

She tilted her head and studied the tight lines etched across his forehead. "What's wrong? Did someone find Bill?"

"No, but they found his truck."

Marie bounced on her toes, the motion causing her to lean forward into Owen's personal space. The scent of pine and lemon wafted from his too-close body. "If he's hurt and doesn't have a truck, he can't be far."

Owen ran a hand through his hair, and the tousled strands poked out in every direction. "He could be with the other guy from the video. An accomplice moving a corpse probably won't blink an eye at harboring a fugitive. Hell, they're both criminals now."

Disappointment dropped her feet to the floor. "Bill's been a criminal for a while."

Owen lowered his chin until his gaze locked on hers. "I'll find him. Stay here, and if you need anything call me."

She flitted her gaze to the end of the hall. "Okay."

Owen ran a long finger along his jawline. "I hate leaving you, but Pappy's here. He can help with anything you need."

A pang of emotion squeezed her heart. These two men—the one in front of her and the old man who shot a man to save her and her baby—were strangers. Yet they had offered her shelter, protection, and hope. Her chin wobbled, and she bit into her top lip to stop herself from doing something stupid—like blubbering and making a fool of herself. "Thanks."

Owen tucked in his lips, a smile tilting up his mouth. "Gotta run."

He turned to slide past her in the narrow hall, and she took a step back so his body wouldn't brush against hers. Her nerve endings sang from his nearness. No telling what would happen if his toned, sexy shoulder connected with her skin. She sighed and watched him, allowing the sizzle of hormones to fizzle out.

Opening the front door, Owen glanced over his shoulder and flashed his dimples once more before disappearing.

Marie leaned against the floral wallpaper in the hall and pressed a hand to her heart. She had to get a grip. Her future needed figured out, and she couldn't do that if she swooned every time the hottie deputy was near.

Straightening on a sigh, she glanced toward Lewis' room. He still sat hunched over his computer. Whatever he watched, she didn't want to see. Maybe now was a good time to steal a few minutes and call her sister. As much as her heart hurt without Nora near, she could actually sit and concentrate to a conversation for the first time in months with her safely back at the shelter.

She hurried to the quiet kitchen. The cool tile on the kitchen floor seeped into the bottoms of her bare feet. She glanced around the cluttered room. Dark brown liquid filled the coffee pot on the counter, coffee grounds scattered around the machine. High stacks of papers sat on the island and made the granite underneath almost impossible to see. A layer of dust coated the oak cabinets and dirty dishes towered in the sink.

Shaking her head, she sank onto a backless stool at the island and plucked the pre-paid phone from her pocket. She punched in the number to reach her sister and lifted the phone to her ear. After she checked in with Renee, she'd give Lewis' house a good cleaning while she waited for Owen to return and take her back to the shelter. Making his home shine and taking away the stale smell of dirt and old food was the least she could do.

Her heart pounded in her chest with every ring. *Please answer the phone.*

"Hello?" A hint of a question lifted the cadence of Renee's words.

"Renee, it's Marie."

"Seriously? Oh my gosh. Marie! How are you? How's my niece? Where are you? I've been worried sick."

Her sister's husky voice shook, and Marie tightened her grip on the phone. She could picture her sister's wide green eyes, so much like her own, and her blonde hair that made them look so different. She hated that her sister had been worried, but she had no way of getting in contact with her.

Besides, it was better Renee remained oblivious of her situation. She had one more year of high school to finish, and Marie would do everything in her power to make sure Renee had a chance of a better future. One filled with college and crushes and dreams—not heartbreak and regret and an obligation to take care of everyone but herself.

The time had come for Marie to tell Renee what had happened. At least enough to put her on alert. "I'm sorry I haven't gotten a hold of you. It's been…difficult. But you need to know what's happened. I need to know you and Mom are safe."

"What do you mean? What's going on?"

She sucked in a deep breath. Best to dive right in. "Bill's gotten himself into some trouble."

Renee snorted. "Big surprise. I don't know why you're with that loser."

Marie cringed at the nasty edge to her sister's voice. She hadn't told Renee about the trouble their mother had gotten into, and how Marie's leaving town with Bill was the only way to protect them all. The seven-year age gap, not to mention her mother's instability and father's non-existence in their lives, made Marie more of a parent figure to Renee than a sister sometimes. "I didn't have much of a choice."

"You always have a choice."

Marie smiled. Renee's wisdom never ceased to amaze her, even if she was a bit naïve. "Not this time, but that's not the point. Bill's on the run, and I'm worried he'll head back home. If he does, there's no telling what he'll do. I need you to make sure the doors are always locked, and Mom doesn't do anything stupid."

"Has anyone ever stopped Mom from making dumb decisions?"

"How has she been since I left?" The idea of Renee being alone with their mom was a hard pill to swallow, but Renee could take care of herself for the most part. Even if their mom had a history of drug use, it was better for Renee to have their mom home than in jail...or worse, dead. Her mom had promised to clean up her act after she narrowly avoided jail time and was put on probation.

"Actually, pretty decent. I really think she's going to stay clean this time."

Relief loosened the knot of anxiety taking up residence in the pit of her stomach...but only a fraction. "Good to hear."

Creak

Marie straightened and leaned toward the doorway, glancing down the hall. Lewis hadn't emerged from his room. The noise must have been the old house shifting.

A tiny thud sounded behind her, and she jumped to her feet. "Renee, I got to go."

"But—"

"I'll call soon." Marie hung up and raised the phone in the air. She tiptoed toward the family room, searching for either the source of the noise or a better weapon than a stupid phone.

Meow

A black cat circled around the leg of the table, wrapping its tail along the wood. Marie let out a shaky breath and set down the phone on the table. She bent low on her heels and held out her hand, letting the cat ram its pink nose against the tips of her fingers. "You silly thing. You scared me half to death." She scooped the cat into her arms and nuzzled her close, reveling in the soft fur against her skin.

A harsh cackle alerted her to someone else's presence, and she glanced over her shoulder into Bill's hateful brown eyes. "Get off the floor. You're coming with me."

THE CALL of crickets sang from between the towering trees. The outline of the Smoky Mountains loomed in the distance. Flies buzzed around Owen's head, no doubt attracted by the stench of sweat collecting under his shirt. The sun beat down from the cloudless sky, causing heat waves to shimmer above the black asphalt on the country road.

Two patrol cars parked on the side of the street, and he rounded them to find Tommy, his dad, and Deputy Stacey Clowman crouched low with their gazes focused on the ground beside the abandoned red truck.

"What do you got?" He narrowed his gaze but couldn't make out what held their attention from his vantage point.

All three stood and faced him.

"Second set of tread marks. Thanks to the rain from yesterday, it's easy to see the other tire tracks." Mike sunk back to his spot beside the truck and trailed his index finger along the ground. "Second set is smaller. Probably a sedan of some kind. Came off the road beside the truck, pulled out the way it came in."

Owen drew closer to his dad and studied the marks. He had little doubt his father was wrong, but he'd need to call in the crime scene unit to run the treads. Maybe they'd get more specific information on what type of tires to look for, even if they weren't yet sure what car Bill had now—or who he was with. "Have you looked inside the truck?"

Stacey nodded and secured her sunglasses on her pert nose. Her auburn hair was pulled back in a stubby ponytail. "I checked the registration in the glovebox. Everything I found was in Bill Flanders' name."

Owen peered inside the half-open window. "Don't see a lot of blood."

"No, sir. Either the guy got patched up, or his injury wasn't that serious." Stacey retrieved a pair of rubber gloves from her front pocket and handed them to Owen. "Might be a bit small, but they'll work."

"Thanks, and good find. We'll take it from here."

Stacey tightened her jaw, nodded, then headed back to her cruiser and drove away.

Tommy shook his head. "Doesn't make sense. Pappy always says if you're gonna take a shot, you better make it count. He wouldn't have grazed the guy just to scare him off, and Pappy has the best aim of anyone I know."

"I called every hospital within a twenty-mile radius this morning," Owen said and squeezed his hands into the gloves before opening the door of the truck. "No one with a gunshot wound came in last night. But you're right, Tommy, Pappy normally wouldn't have missed. But it was dark, and he shot down a ravine. It'd be a tough shot for anyone."

A mess of receipts and crumpled fast-food bags were scattered along the floor of Bill's truck.

Owen cringed. Judging by the smell, a half-eaten cheeseburger probably filled one of the sacks. The passenger door swung open, and Owen glanced over to find the steady eyes of his dad taking in the clutter. "Pappy showed me footage of the woods last night. Two men carrying a woman to the river."

"So, the scumbag has a friend willing to help hide a murder victim then dump his truck in the woods." Mike shifted through the papers with glove-covered hands, smoothing out receipts and placing them in a pile on the leather seat.

"Yep. We need to find out who this guy runs around with." He glanced over his shoulder. "Any word on who owns the house?"

"I checked the auditor's website," Tommy said. "The land was last purchased two years ago by a developer, Piper Properties. Owned by Steven Piper. I put in a call to him, but he didn't answer."

"Why would Pappy sell off parts of his land to a developer? Doesn't make any sense." Owen patted the worn seat and slipped his fingers along the cracks. Nothing but crumbs and dirt sprung from the spot where the seat met the backrest.

Mike grunted. "Who knows why that crazy old man does half the stuff he does—cameras all over the woods, alarms covering the house and property. I wouldn't be surprised if he has bear traps hidden on the forest floor in case some unknowing soul has the nerve to step in his yard."

Owen wanted to argue but couldn't. "Whatever his reasons, we need to talk to Steven Piper if he owns the house this guy lives in," Owen said, ignoring his dad's comments about Pappy.

After his mother had been killed, his grandfather had barely kept his grasp on reality, his mind always caught between moving on and a fierce need to close the case that took his only child's life. His granny had been the only one capable of keeping Lewis from becoming completely consumed with seeking justice.

When she'd passed away a few years ago, Lewis slipped further and further into a pit of despair that no one could pull him out of. Most days, Lewis didn't leave the cave of memories, research, and depression he called a bedroom. Owen tried to suck up his own misery over the events that had stolen his mother a decade before and be there for his grandfather, but the old man didn't make it easy—clinging to a past Owen didn't want to remember and constantly berating Owen's father at the same time. Most days, it was too much to deal with.

"Did you get any answers from the girl?" Mike hiked a knee on the floor of the truck, squeezing his heavy frame between the bench seat and the dashboard.

Marie's confession back at the shelter floated into his mind. The past she'd revealed was part of the investigation and could be crucial to finding Bill before he hurt anyone else, but he didn't want to tell all of her secrets.

Not all of it was necessary for them to do their jobs.

"Found out the guy used video he took of Marie's mom selling drugs to blackmail her into leaving town with him. She said he's been into some bad stuff for a while, but never mentioned any arrest. We need to touch base with the police from her hometown and see if they can shed any light."

Tommy appeared behind Mike and shoved his hands in his pockets. "Do you think she could be involved in any of this? Even if she isn't connected to the murder, what are the chances this girl was unaware of what he had going on? Seems to me she'd know where he'd hide better than anyone."

Owen shifted to get a better angle under the steering wheel. He skimmed his fingers along the plastic of the column then turned to glance under the seat. "I'll check into her more when I get a chance, but my gut says to trust her. Besides, she's been consumed with taking care of her baby—with keeping her safe."

Mike chuckled. "Must be a good-looking girl for you to believe her so easily."

Owen gritted his teeth and kept his opinions to himself. True, he didn't usually trust people based on their word, but there was something different about Marie. Something that warned him to be careful. Not because he couldn't trust her, but because he could fall for her way too easy.

Jamming his hand under the seat, his fingers slid across

something sticky on the floor and Owen shuddered. He flipped up his palm, and his hand brushed against a bulky object adhered to the bottom of the seat.

"Found something." Pinching together his fingers, he grabbed the object and pulled it from beneath the seat. His shoulder screamed at the awkward angle, and he backed out of the truck and stood tall to stretch his achy muscles.

Footsteps hurried toward him as he studied the items in his hands. "Pills. Possibly opioids."

Mike and Tommy gathered close.

"Guys carting drugs around in his truck, then leaves it all behind for us to find? Is he an idiot or what?" Tommy huffed out a humorless laugh.

"I don't know. Could be he's in a hurry to get out of town and doesn't care what we found. He knows he's screwed, and a little bit of drugs is nothing compared to murder." Owen lifted the baggie in the air and tried to decipher the markings engraved on the little white pills. "Or it could be something else."

"What other reason is there?"

Owen lowered the bag and fear grabbed hold of his heart. "The only way to lure us away from where he wants to be."

8

Marie stayed low to the ground and hugged the cat tight. Her heart raced, and for the first time since leaving Nora behind, she was glad she'd entrusted her new friends with her baby's safety.

Bill stood in front of the wide-open door that led to the back deck. Dried blood stained his white tank top and a yellow pallor glistened under his stubbled jaw. Mud streaked through his tawny hair. A gun rested in his hand, dangling at his side as if he didn't think he'd actually have to use it—as though she wouldn't dare fight back.

She rose to her feet and tensed her muscles. She was tired of being bossed around. A brief idea flashed of throwing the fat cat at his face and running, but she couldn't bring herself to endanger the innocent pet. Without taking her eyes off Bill, she placed the cat on the floor then faced him with a narrowed gaze.

The cat arched her back and hissed, backing into her legs.

Bill jerked his body forward with his hands in the air. "Hiissss."

A deep growl vibrated from the cat's throat then she ran into the other room.

Bill laughed. "Stupid cat." He took a step forward and glanced around the room. "How'd you worm your way into this setup? Spread your legs for him, too? I'd just love to say hello. I owe him a little payback before we leave."

The last thing she wanted to do was leave with Bill, but she couldn't let him hurt Lewis. Not after everything he'd done for her. She needed to get Bill out of the house quickly. She'd figure out how to get away from him once they had put some distance between him and Lewis. "You don't want to mess with him. His grandson's working the case of the woman you killed last night."

Bill sneered. "You don't think I know that? I don't go anywhere without doing my homework, and I know all about the crazy old man who lives here."

Marie lifted her chin. "Then you know he's not a threat. But his grandson is, and he'll be back any minute."

Bill took another step forward. "All the reason to hurry."

Bile slid up her throat, but she couldn't let him see her fear. He fed off of it, and she needed to be strong. For herself, and for Lewis. "I'll go where you want. Just leave him out of this."

Eyeing her up and down, Bill latched on to her bicep and yanked her to him. "I'll do whatever I want. Grab Nora while I take care of the old man."

"No, what you're going to do is leave her alone. Now." Lewis stood in the doorway with his shotgun aimed at Bill. "If you move, I'll shoot you again."

Laughing, Bill pulled her in front of him like a shield and pressed his gun to the tender flesh of her side. "I don't think so. I've got a man out front waiting for us, and if you try anything stupid, I'll make sure my bullet does a lot more damage to her than yours did to me."

Lewis tilted his head to the side. "If you know anything

about me, you'd know no one would pull into my driveway without alerting me."

Bill snorted and twisted the barrel of the gun against her shirt, the hard edge biting into her skin. She leaned away from the gun, and her elbow connected with Bill's side.

He hissed out a breath and lowered his mouth to her ear. "Stop. Moving."

His breath landed like hot, muggy air against her cheek, and she fought the urge to swipe it from her face.

Marie locked gazes with Lewis for a beat. Lewis tilted his chin toward Bill's side—the same spot she'd brushed against. She dropped her gaze to the gun Bill had pressed against her. Bill had the weapon trained above her left hip, which meant he was holding the gun with his nondominant hand. His right hand must be injured or too weak to use.

Closing her eyes, Marie weighed her options. Lewis would never let Bill take her, and Bill wouldn't allow Lewis to live if he could hand over evidence of Bill's getaway car. She needed to get away from Bill and keep Lewis safe. She opened her eyes, blew a breath through barely parted lips, and jammed her elbow into Bill's injured side.

"Sonofa..." Bill released his grip. He doubled over and swung his left arm through the air to cradle his injury. Bill's gun erupted.

The deafening sound beat against her ear drum, and Marie fell to the floor.

"I'll make you pay." Bill straightened, but his shoulders dropped forward.

Fear sank its fangs in her throat. Marie glanced at the doorway.

Lewis lay on the floor, his gun by his side.

Marie scurried to her feet and lunged for the weapon. She turned, squeezing the barrel of the gun between her hands and locked her sight on Bill.

Blood soaked through his shirt and coated his fingers. The gun remained in his left hand and aimed at her head, but his arm hung at an odd angle.

Her body shook, making the gun in her hands bob up and down. Every fiber of her being screamed to shoot him, to make him pay for the sins he'd committed. Her breath came out in spasms, and she couldn't stop her stupid toe from tap, tap, tapping against the tile.

A slow smile slid onto Bill's narrow mouth. "You don't got it in you to kill me. Besides, I'll finish off the old man if you make any move at all."

Marie spared a quick glance at Lewis. Blood pooled on the floor beneath him, but she couldn't take her focus off Bill long enough to find out how badly he'd been injured.

"I'm going to walk out the way I came. You're going to stay right there." Bill took one slow step backward, then another, toward the door with his gun trained on Lewis.

Adrenaline coursed through her veins. She kept her arms straight, never taking her gaze from Bill's retreating form. She longed to squeeze the trigger, but she'd never shot a gun in her life. It couldn't be as easy as it looked in the movies, especially with her nerves bouncing around her body. And if she missed, she had no doubt Bill would stay true to his word and kill Lewis.

As much as she hated to stand there and watch him leave, it was her only option.

A blare of a horn honked from outside and an engine revved. A blue car cut through the back yard, visible through the open door. The driver cranked the wheel so the car spun through the grass and faced the way it had just come. Someone pushed open the passenger door.

Bill puckered his lips and kissed the air. "See you and our daughter soon, Babe." He fled through the door at a half run, half shuffle and stumbled into the car.

A sob tore through Marie and she dropped to the floor, releasing the gun from her death grip. Lewis laid on his stomach, his eyes closed and his entire body still. Dark crimson oozed through the denim of his jeans. Marie had no experience with first aid and logic didn't compute in her muddled mind.

She jumped to her feet and grabbed the phone from the table. Her fingers trembled as she pressed 9-1-1 and held the phone to her ear.

"9-1-1. What's your emergency?"

"A man's been shot." Marie dropped back down next to Lewis and placed her fingers along the inside of his wrist. "He has a pulse, but he's old and weak. He needs help now."

"Okay. Where are you?"

Panic flooded her brain. She didn't know Lewis' address. "In a house by the river. Just north of town. Lewis Sinclair's house."

A sharp gasp rattled the speaker. "I'm sending a squad there now. Please stay on the line until they get there."

Adrenaline fled her body, and her teeth clattered together. She cradled her palm around Lewis' limp hand. "I need the police here, too. The man who shot him is wanted for murder, and he just drove away."

OWEN WAITED at the four-way stop in front of the pedestrian walkway along the red brick road that cut down the center of town. He tapped his index finger against the top of the steering wheel as a young mother led her toddler to the other side of the street toward the ice cream shop on the corner.

The little boy hopped beside his mother, a wide grin plastered across his cherub face.

Owen fought the urge to yell to them to hurry. He hated to drive through town where the speed limit slowed him down, but it was still quicker than cutting around the edge of the city limits.

Pressing his foot on the gas pedal, he lurched forward and headed toward Pappy's. He had work to do, but a nagging sensation in his gut told him to check in. He'd tried calling, but no one had answered, which only increased his anxiety.

The sound of sirens in the distance perked his ears, and he glanced into the rearview mirror. Angry slashes of red and blue bled against the bright sky. He pulled to the side of the road and turned up the volume of the police scanner on his dashboard. Noise crackled and voices crashed, calling out codes and locations. Nothing that needed the parade of emergency vehicles barreling toward him.

His phone rang, and he glanced at the screen before answering. His sister hardly ever called in the middle of the day. Sweat moistened his palms as he accepted the call. "Hey, Katherine. What's up?" An ambulance and two patrol cars sped past. Not waiting to find out what happened, he slid onto the bumpy road and followed behind the patrol car.

"Owen, where are you?" Katherine's panicked voice pounded against his eardrum.

"Downtown, following a couple cops and an ambulance." He squinted, trying to make out the driver of the police car. "They sped by me on my way to Pappy's. I want to find out where they're going."

"Get to Pappy's. Now. They're probably on their way here."

Owen straightened and tightened his grip on the wheel. "What happened?" Following in the wake of the screaming sirens meant no traffic blocked his path, but he added pressure to the gas pedal to get as close as he could to the car in front of him. Icy blasts of fear shot up his spine.

"Pappy was shot."

Owen fought not to crush his eyes closed as his body took the physical impact of her words. "Is he okay?" His throat almost closed around the question, but he needed to know what to expect when he arrived at his grandfather's house—an injured old man or a dead body.

"He's alive. I'm more concerned about the bump on his head than the bullet wound. The bullet grazed his leg. But he fell and hit his head, knocked him out for a while."

Relief cleared the thickness in his throat, but more questions flooded his brain. "Why are you there?"

"I got a call from the dispatcher—she's a friend of mine. I came straight here and made it before anyone else. Some woman's here, too. Said she knows you." A film of weariness coated Katherine's distress. "She's pretty shaken up. Some guy named Bill showed up. He shot Pappy when she tried to get away from him." A tremor sliced through her voice.

Owen smacked the heel of his hand against the steering wheel, and the horn blared. "I got to make a call. The ambulance should be there soon. I'm right behind them."

Ending the call, Owen unleashed a growl of frustration. He'd been right. Bill had stranded his truck where it would easily be found to lure him away from Marie. The bastard had stayed close enough to keep an eye on her since last night, and Owen had played right into his hand—leaving not only Marie, but Pappy, exposed to a lunatic.

At least the baby hadn't been there.

The red brick ended, and his car sailed on the smooth asphalt toward Pappy's house. The road curved alongside the river, the water higher than normal after the constant rain the last few days. Owen needed both hands to keep his vehicle steady as he raced. He activated the voice command on the wheel. "Call Tommy."

Ringing blared through the speakers while Owen kept his gaze focused ahead.

"Hey. What's up?" Tommy's voice boomed in the car.

"I need you and Dad at Pappy's. Bill showed up and shot Pappy. I don't have many details, but Katherine's there now."

"Is Pappy all right?"

"Katherine said she thinks he'll be fine, and I trust her judgement. But he's old, and there's no telling what an injury like this could do."

Muttered curses dominated the phone line. "The bastard played us."

"Looks like it. If we're lucky, Pappy got something on video to help us figure out which way he went. We need to move quickly."

"Dad and I are on our way. We're still at the truck, so it won't take long."

Owen veered off the road onto Pappy's long driveway. The canopy of tall trees branching over the lane blocked out the sun and cast a shadow over his car. The brick ranch where he'd spent so much of his childhood came into view, and a flood of memories crashed into him. He might trust Katherine's opinion, but he needed to see Pappy...then he needed to find the man who'd hurt him. "I'm here now. See you soon."

Clicking off the line, Owen pulled into a small patch of stones on the edge of the driveway. The EMTs didn't need him blocking them in when it was time to take Pappy to the hospital. He slammed on the brakes, and gravel pinged against the side of his vehicle. He drew in a deep breath, shut off the engine, and jumped from the car. He ran across the yard, dashed up the porch, and charged inside.

A circus might as well be crammed in the small living room. Pappy sat on the floor with his legs straight in front of him and his back pressed against the sofa. Katherine sat beside him, her red-rimmed eyes focused on their grandfather and blond hair pulled behind her shoulders in a low ponytail. An EMT kneeled beside Pappy, checking vitals and arguing something in a low voice.

Owen closed the short distance to his grandpa and dropped beside him. "Are you okay? What happened?"

A sheen of perspiration coated Lewis' thin skin, and he winced as he shifted to face Owen. "I was at my desk and heard the alarm go off. I came out with my shotgun, but the scumbag grabbed Marie and used her as a shield."

Guilt and anger swirled inside Owen's veins. He clenched his jaw and balled his hands into fists. "How did you get shot?"

Lewis raised his brows and the deep wrinkles on his face nearly folded into themselves. "If you'd let me talk, I'd tell you."

Owen laughed. If Pappy had his tough-as-nails attitude and feisty comebacks at the ready, he'd be just fine. "Sorry. Go on."

"I came out and pointed my gun at the guy. Marie—she's smart, I'll give her that—she must have figured out where the guy's injury was. Rammed him in the side, took him by surprise. He swung his arm around to cradle where she'd hit him, and his gun went off. Not sure if he meant to or not, but the bullet hit me on the side of the leg." Lewis rubbed the top of his thigh.

Owen's gaze followed the motion of Lewis' gnarled fingers, and his stomach dropped. Blood coated his worn jeans. He moved his tongue over the dryness of his mouth, unable to form words.

"He's lost some blood. I'd like to take him to the emergency room." The medical worker looped a stethoscope around his neck. "I'm worried about the bump on his head, too. He needs to go to the hospital."

Lewis pressed against the couch and clenched his teeth, shifting his weight in an effort to get to his feet. "I'm not going anywhere."

Katherine flattened a palm on Lewis' shoulder and eased him back to the floor. "Pappy, they need to look at you. We need to make sure you're all right."

"You already gave me a look over, and I'm fine. Now get this crap out of my house." Lewis threw his hand wide, indicating the gurney and medical equipment scattered around.

"Pappy this isn't just a scrape or bruise. You were shot." Owen admired the old man's spunk, but some things were non-negotiable. And going to the hospital to get a gunshot wound looked at was one of them.

Lewis shook his head. "No."

Owen rose, crossed his arms over his chest, and stared down at Lewis. Katherine stood to join him, and dammit if her hard stare and tightly pressed together lips made his five-foot five-inch sister look tougher than him.

"You two can stand there looking like spoiled brats. I'm not going." Lewis stared ahead, ignoring everyone in the room.

"Sir, we need to clean your wound and possibly give you a few stitches." The EMT sighed and rubbed his forehead, making the doughy flesh ripple.

Lewis shrugged. "Clean it here, then."

The emergency worker tightened his jaw, and his tanned face turned red. "I could clean it, but I can't give you sutures."

"Fine. But I'm not staying the night," Lewis said on a sigh.

A soft knock sounded at the door, and Tommy rushed in with Mike at his heels. "Pappy, are you all right?"

Lewis rolled his eyes. "Did you call the whole darn town? I'm fine. These worrywarts are making me get checked out. A waste of time if you ask me."

"Can you ride in the ambulance with him, Katherine? I don't want him to be alone, but I've got my hands full right now." Owen steeled himself for a remark from Pappy, but he wouldn't be swayed. He had more important issues to handle than the ego of an old man. Time ticked by, and Bill got further from his reach with every passing second.

Lewis gritted his teeth and tried to stand. "I don't need a babysitter."

Tommy hurried to Lewis' side and hooked an arm around

his waist, then helped him to the gurney taking up the middle of the living room. "No one says you do. But Katherine can make sure they don't poke and prod you more than necessary."

Owen bit back a smile. Leave it to Tommy to use his charm and good nature to maneuver Pappy where they wanted him.

"Fine." Lewis grumbled and sat on the starched white sheets on the portable bed. "Look at the video feed from the front camera. The jerk bragged about some idiot driving him here."

A bit of pressure released in his chest. If they could find out who this guy ran around with, they could find Bill. "I'll pull it up right now."

Lewis laid flat on the gurney and closed his eyes. The wrinkles of his face appeared to pull downward, aging him ten years since this morning. Fear squeezed his heart. Even if Pappy's leg was fine, an ordeal like this could take much more away from him than Pappy would ever admit. "And don't leave the girl alone. He still wants her. Can't let her down like my Lillian."

Owen sucked in a sharp breath, and his gaze sought his dad. Mike sank onto the floral sofa his grandparents had owned since before Owen could remember and closed his eyes, tightening his jaw. Owen didn't say another word as the medical worker wheeled the gurney to the stoop, and Tommy helped lower the bed to the ground and get the gurney in the back of the ambulance.

Tension sizzled in the air, but Owen couldn't do anything about that now. "Okay. Dad, I need you to watch the footage and see if there are any shots of the car. I need to take Marie's statement."

Marie. Owen needed to talk to her, find out what happened, make sure she was all right.

He stepped into the next room to search for her. She sat with her elbows propped on the table, her faced tipped down.

Stacey sat beside her with a notebook in hand, talking softly and asking questions.

"Marie?"

Her head shot up and the raw emotion in her eyes stole his ability to breathe. Moisture trailed down her cheeks and dark circles hung low under her puffy eyes. He closed the distance between them in three long strides, pulled her to her feet, and folded his arms around her.

She clung to him, grasping his shirt in her hands.

He ran a hand up and down her back as her body shook against his. He shouldn't have left her, made it easy for Bill to sweep in and try to take her. He'd find the bastard and make him pay.

His stomach muscles clenched. The more time he spent with Marie, the harder it would be to forget about her when she went on with her life and he stayed in Water's Edge—alone, the only commitment he could make to a job he loved.

9

Marie slipped onto the back deck. She's spoken with Deputy Clowman and Owen and now she needed a little space. Her heart ached to hold her baby close. To breath in the familiar scents of baby shampoo and lotion. But the last thing she wanted was to ask for a ride home and get in the way of Owen's investigation.

Especially after she was the reason Lewis was shot.

Sitting on the squeaky glider, she stared into the dense woods. It was hard to believe it was just the night before she had scurried up the steep banks, running for her life. Nora pressed to her chest and pure terror spurring her forward. Dirt still lingered under her long fingernails, her quick shower earlier not enough to erase evidence of her escape through the muddy terrain.

A shiver ripped down her spine despite the heat. Now she had another bad memory to add to the others of Bill. Her nerves still shuddered, and she needed the warm rays of the sun to chase away the lingering bits of fear before she could head back inside and figure out her next move.

Yearning squeezed her chest. She wished her next move included a man like Owen Wells.

Warmth engulfed her at the memory of being wrapped in his arms. No one had ever held her like that, wanting only to offer her comfort and strength and safety, demanding nothing in return.

The back door squeaked open, and Marie glanced behind her shoulder and into Owen's hazel eyes. The sun shone bright overhead, and Owen squinted against the harsh light.

"There you are. Mind if I take a seat?" He dipped his chin toward the glider and slid a backpack from his back to drop it by his feet.

She scooted over, shifting to tuck her feet under her. Despite the desperate situation they'd fallen into, all she wanted was to lean forward and press her lips to his—to feel his arms around her again as they sat cuddled on a cozy glider surrounded by the songs of spring.

She dropped her gaze to her hands. She had to stop seeing Owen as more than what he was...an officer of the law doing his job. Besides, even if she wanted to try for something more once this nightmare was behind her, what could she possibly offer a man like Owen? Another man's child? A woman with no education, no life goals beyond survival? "So, what's next?"

"We need to search the woods. Bill fled in a car, but since there's no other sign of where he went, I want to make sure he isn't holed up out here." Leaning forward, he clasped his hands and rested his forearms on his knees. "My brother is here and can help while my dad goes over the surveillance footage."

Marie nodded.

He turned his head to glance at her, concern and a little bit of guilt shining from his eyes. "I know you probably want to get back to the shelter, but we need to move quick on this. I can have someone else drive you, if you'd like."

The thought of trusting yet another person sat like a boulder in her chest. "I'd rather wait for you."

"Okay," he said, and she swore he tried to hide a glimpse of a smile. "Why don't you head out with me and Tommy? You can be an extra set of eyes while we search the woods."

She mustered a smile. The woods held a ton of bad memories, but somehow knowing Owen would be by her side made facing her nightmares easier. "Let's go."

The backdoor swung open again, and a deputy with a clean-shaven face and eyes the same color as Owen's stepped outside.

Owen stood. "Marie, this is my brother, Tommy."

Tommy dipped his chin in greeting. "We ready?"

Owen nodded, swung his bag over his shoulders, and followed Tommy down the steps and over the small patch of grass toward the woods.

Marie sucked in a deep breath and scurried behind them.

Mosquitoes buzzed around Marie's ear, and she swatted them away as she descended deeper into the forest. Mud squelched under her sneakers as she followed Owen and Tommy, coating the once-white material in dark brown stains. Each step was harder than the last, her feet either sticking in the muck or sliding over wet grass.

"Doing all right back there?" Owen asked with a quick glance over his shoulder.

She wiped off beads of sweat at her hairline. How had she managed this with Nora? "I'm fine. Just not used to hiking. Should I be looking for anything specific?"

"Anything that grabs your attention or doesn't look like it belongs. It's a long shot to find something, but I'd rather take a quick look just in case."

A rustle of leaves sounded to her right, and Marie paused, searching through the dense brush for what caused the commotion. A chipmunk darted from under the mound of vibrant green vegetation and took off down the riverbank. "Holy crap." Marie placed a hand over her thundering heart and leaned against the rough bark of a tall tree.

"Tommy, hold up," Owen hollered then hurried to her side. "What is it? Are you okay?"

Marie laughed at her own stupidity and shook her head, raising her eyes to the patches of blue sky that broke through the covering of trees. "Sorry. A chipmunk just scared me to death. Guess I'm not much of a nature girl."

Owen hoisted the backpack he carried high on his shoulders and grinned. "Those hairy little beasts can be terrifying if you're a gardener, but otherwise they're harmless."

Marie rolled her eyes. "I'm not afraid of chipmunks. I heard it rummaging around and didn't know what it was until it shot out in front of me." She pushed off the tree and kicked around the tall blades of grass and clumps of wet leaves.

A long red feather with thick black stripes caught her attention. She bent low for a closer look. "What an unusual feather. That's not from a cardinal, is it?"

Owen crouched beside her and reached for it.

"Don't pick it up. Bird feathers are infested with bugs and disease." She shuddered. The feather may be beautiful, no matter what kind of bird it came from, but no way she'd let it touch her.

"I don't think it's from a bird at all." Owen lowered his pack, unzipped the front, and pulled out a pair of gloves. He fit his hands into the gloves then picked up the feather. "Hey, Tommy. Come look at this."

The crunch of sticks and twigs preceded Tommy and echoed through the stillness of the quiet woods. Even the birds were noiseless this morning, probably trying to catch up on the sleep the storm from last night had interrupted.

"What is it?" Tommy pinched together his forehead and leaned over Owen's shoulder.

Owen held up the feather. "Is this from an arrow?"

Tommy dropped beside Owen and studied the feather. "Looks like it. See how it narrows down to a point on one end? This would go on one side of the back of the arrow, two more around it."

Marie took a closer look. She could see now how the shape and pattern on the feather were too perfect, too exact. "I thought the feathers that came from an arrow were synthetic and all one color?"

Tommy shrugged and rose. "Depends on the type of bow someone's using. Most people use crossbows to hunt. They're more efficient. But there are still people who prefer to use a more primitive bow and make their arrows. It takes a lot more time and effort, but for some, taking pride in the arrows they make is half the fun."

She tilted her head and studied Owen's brother. "Do you hunt?" She couldn't hide the skepticism in her voice. The hunters she knew from home had large, bushy beards and always wore camouflage. Tommy was as clean-cut as a child, and his uniform was pressed to perfection.

He chuckled. "Not anymore. Owen and I used to come out here when we were kids. I'd come alone after he left the house. Always liked being in the woods."

"Well, I don't like that someone's been hunting without permission," Owen said, standing. "Think we can track where this was bought?" He waved the feather in the air.

Tommy twisted his lips. "Every hunter has their own style, but the materials they use are mass produced. Water's Edge has a couple of specialty stores we can check, but someone could just as easily buy supplies online."

Marie bounced her gaze from one man to the other. "I get why you don't want people trespassing, but why does it matter who the feather belongs to?" She wasn't a detective, but they had more important matters to uncover than finding who'd bought a stupid feather.

"Might be worth looking into," Owen said. "If someone has been out here recently, they might have seen something useful."

Tommy stepped closer to the tree and roamed his hand up and down the trunk. "Some fairly fresh divots on the bark. How far do you think we are from Pappy's house?"

Owen turned a wide circle. "About a mile. We're near the property line now, but then the patch of land on the other side that Steven Piper bought belongs to Pappy as well. That's what I'm the most interested in searching. Pappy would have spied anything out of the norm closer to home."

"If we're close to Bill's house, maybe he bought the feathers." Tommy glanced at Marie. "Is he a hunter?"

Marie snorted. "No. He always carries a gun with him, but not the hunting kind and mostly to make himself look tough."

The memory of Bill jamming the gun in her side then shooting Lewis sprang to life in her mind, and she winced. Bill had shown her he was capable of more than she ever thought possible, but spending time and resources making his own arrows for fun didn't seem like a possibility.

Owen nodded and tucked the feather into his bag, leaving the gloves in place. "Let's keep moving."

Minutes ticked by and the air heated even more. The sound of the river lapping against the bank rolled in her ears. Thirst parched her dry throat, and the desire to peel off her clothes and jump in the water nearly overwhelmed her.

She marched onward, scanning the forest floor for anything of interest. The cry of a hawk squalled above her, and she glanced up, searching the overhang of branches for the bird. A dark silhouette formed in the trees.

Marie jolted to a stop and shielded her eyes with her hand. "Guys? What is that?" She pointed toward the hut-like structure secured on a wooden platform about twenty feet off the ground, green and brown chipped paint on its sides. Excitement and fear bubbled in her chest.

She might have just found Bill's hiding spot.

OWEN STOPPED and pivoted toward Marie, aiming his glance to where the tip of her finger pointed. An old treehouse perched between the thick branches above him. A wave of nostalgia so strong barreled into him, he almost doubled over. He whirled in the opposite direction. Tommy was several yards ahead.

"Tommy, come here." A wide smile slid onto Owen's face, and he locked eyes with Marie then gestured toward the tree she pointed at with a nod of his head. "You found our old hunting blind."

Marie hurried to his side, her long ponytail swinging with the motion. "Your what?"

He chuckled. "Our hunting blind. It's a place you sit and hide when you're hunting so the animals don't see you."

Marie shuddered and glanced up at the shabby hut. "So, you sit there just waiting for something to come along you can shoot? Seems cruel."

A bite of guilt shimmied into his gut. "Well, when you put it like that..."

She studied him, her lips screwed to the side and nose scrunched. "I didn't figure you for a hunter. You asked Tommy about the feather. Do you not use a bow?"

Owen rubbed a palm over his chin. "Tommy and I didn't do much actual hunting. We just liked having a place to escape. We spent a lot of time at Pappy's when we were younger, and there's nothing better for a kid than a cool fort, an empty patch of land, and a BB gun."

Tommy jogged to his side. "What did you find this time? I keep missing stuff."

A grin spread on Owen's mouth, and he raised his eyes toward the raggedy pile of boards he hadn't stepped foot on for years.

"Holy cow," Tommy said on a laugh. "I can't believe that thing is still standing. Do you think those old nudie magazines are still up there?"

Owen gritted his teeth and gave Tommy a hard stare. Not like it'd help.

Marie shot him an amused smirk and raised her brows. "Sounds like you guys took your hunting really seriously."

Tommy slapped a hand on Owen's back. "Do you remember how mad Katherine used to get when we wouldn't let her up? Looks like the steps are still secured to the tree. Wonder if it'll hold my weight?"

Owen closed the short distance to the tree trunk. The same wide planks of wood Pappy had helped them hammer into the tree sat secure on top of the rough, brown bark. One board sat inches above the next and the next, all the way up to the wide platform anchored around the tree. The blind they'd spent an entire summer assembling and painting sat snuggly against the thick branches, wide green leaves shadowing the structure. The pitched roof still covered the four walls they'd toiled over, taking weeks to fit the material together, then hoist into the tree.

"Can't tell for sure, but it doesn't look like any of the wood's rotted. But if it could hold your weight, it could hold Bill's. We need to check it out. I should do it."

Tommy snorted. "No way I can walk past it and not go up. I'll check it out." Tommy gripped each makeshift step above his head, placing the side of his foot on the wooden planks. "I don't remember it being so difficult to get up here."

Marie took a step closer to Owen and grabbed the shirt

covering his biceps in a tight grip. "Is this safe? What if he falls?"

Owen kept his gaze fixed on Tommy, and his muscles tightened with every step higher his brother took. "Wouldn't be the first time."

Tommy made it to the base of the blind and swung his leg over the side. The old planks shuddered but held in place. Tommy braced his hands on the railing and stared over the woods. "This is surreal. Everything looks the same."

Marie released her grip on his shirt. "He proved he could still make it up there, now tell him to get down. He's making me nervous."

Releasing a pent-up breath, he couldn't help but agree with Marie. He cupped his hands to his mouth and yelled, "Take a quick look then come down. We've got work to do."

Tommy lifted his index finger and grinned. "One second." He disappeared through the thick foliage shielding most of the blind.

Owen chuckled and turned his stare on her. His heart constricted. A cotton tank top may be covering her curves, but the shape of her was imprinted in his mind. His fingers itched to feel her soft, smooth skin again.

Thud!

The platform shook and debris rained from the tree. Panic pounded against Owen's temples. "Tommy! Are you okay?"

No response.

"Oh my God. It sounds like he fell." Fear rose Marie's voice an octave.

"Crap. I told him to come down." Owen dropped the backpack to the ground and ran to the base of the tree. "Tommy, if you're playing around, I'm going to kill you. Answer me, dammit! What's going on?"

More silence.

He steadied his hands on the homemade ladder scaling the

tree. "Stay here," he said to Marie. He hated to leave her alone, even if he was right above her, but he needed to make sure Tommy was all right.

His limbs trembled as he clung to the slivers of moist wood. The tips of his fingers ached as he clung for his life and pushed himself up the tree. He didn't look down, didn't think about what would happen if his foot slipped or one of the old pieces of wood broke free from the trunk. He climbed as fast as he could and breathed a sigh of relief when he reached the platform and hoisted himself on the level floor.

The bottom of Tommy's boot poked from the narrow door to the little hut. He hurried toward Tommy, the rushed movement causing the treehouse to sway. He slowed his paced and dropped to his brother's side.

Tommy lay sprawled on his stomach with his eyes closed and breathing shallow.

What the hell had happened?

Owen swept his gaze around the gloomy space and ice froze his blood.

Bits of busted glass scattered on the ground and pieces of equipment lined a shelf he and Tommy had once used to hold their bags of chips and cans of cola. Crouching so he didn't hit his head on the low ceiling, Owen crossed over to the study the equipment. A Bunsen burner sat tilted on its side and various sized beakers lay beside it.

You've got to be kidding me.

Someone had used their hunting blind as a lab.

Realization dawned on him, and he rushed back to Tommy. Sinking to the balls of his feet, he followed the line of Tommy's outstretched hand. A crate had been pushed against the wall, the tips of Tommy's fingers brushing against the edge. Owen peered over the side of the crate. More shards of glass lined the top of the crate and a thin layer of white powder sprinkled between debris, bits of the powder falling down like dust to the floor.

White powder with this setup could only mean one thing. It was pure, synthetic Fentanyl. If touched with bare skin, it could be fatal.

A fist of fear squeezed Owen's heart. He ran to the railing and stared down at Marie's terror-filled expression. "Tommy touched Fentanyl. He needs Narcan now or he'll die."

10

O wen gripped the splintered wood of the railing and focused on Marie. "Grab the backpack and come up here. Now."

Satisfied Marie could make it safely up the tree, he ran back to Tommy and dropped to his knees. With one hand cradled around his neck, he gently turned him so he laid on his back. Owen placed one trembling hand on Tommy's chin, tilted his head slightly, and pinched his nose. Leaning forward, he sealed his mouth over his brother's and breathed life into him. He needed to keep oxygen in Tommy's brain until he could get the lifesaving drug inside him.

A huff of labored breath preceded Marie over the side of the platform.

Owen released his mouth and glanced at her. "Give me the bag. Hurry."

Thank God he always kept Narcan in his bag. He just never imagined he'd have to use it on his brother.

Marie ripped the bag off her back and threw it toward him.

He caught it one-handed, unzipped the front pouch, and yanked a syringe out of its case. A red cover guarded the pointed tip of the needle, and Owen tore it off. He placed the end against the middle of Tommy's thigh and pressed the device against his leg. A click sounded and a hissing noise vibrated against Owen's hand as the medicine flowed into Tommy.

Time crawled by.

Come on. Don't die on me.

Yanking his phone from his pocket, he called 911. "I've got a deputy down. Accidental exposure to Fentanyl-like substance. Narcan has been administered, but still need assistance."

"Where are you located?"

He closed his eyes and fought the urge to scream. "In the middle of the woods. Property owned by Lewis Sinclair, about four miles north of where his house sits."

A beat of hesitation pulsed on the line. "Okay. Is there any way you can get the officer to an easier point of extraction?"

"I don't know. He hasn't woken yet." Emotion made his throat thick, his words hard to squeeze through the ever-tightening space.

A touch on his shoulder had him glancing to the side. Marie's soft eyes loosened something inside him.

She tilted her head toward Tommy.

Owen whipped back around, catching the tiny flutter of Tommy's eyelids.

Please wake up.

Marie slid her hand down his shoulder to catch his hand in hers. He squeezed her palm, needing her strength to calm his taut nerves. He kept his gaze fixed on Tommy, willing him to open his eyes.

Tommy's eyelids squeezed tight. On a sharp gasp of air, his eyes flew open wide. The dark circles of his pupils almost edged out all the hazel of his eyes, and he turned his head back and forth until his gaze latched onto Owen. "What happened?"

Relief released the tension in his body and he leaned forward, bracing his hands on his knees.

"Sir? Are you still there?"

Owen straightened and brought the phone to his ear, snapping into get-crap-done mode. "He's awake. I can get him to the entrance to the trail off Merie Road, the one just north of Lewis' house. We'll be there as soon as possible."

He disconnected the call and focused on Tommy. The stupid lump remained lodged in his throat, and moisture misted in his eyes. He sniffed, pulling back the tears and emotion and every terrifying thought that had paralyzed him at the idea of losing his brother. "You must have touched Fentanyl or a synthetic opioid substitute someone made. You fell hard and fast. I had to administer Narcan, and now we need to get you out of this tree to meet an ambulance."

Tommy let his eyelids drift shut, as if physically taking in the impact of Owen's words. "Guess that explains why I feel like I was hit by truck. Why did you let me come up here?"

Owen snorted. "Like I could have stopped you."

Tommy was as stubborn as the rest of the family. But Owen should have been the one to go up the tree. He would have been more cautious, known what to look for and what not to touch.

"Dude, I can see those wheels of yours working. You can't blame yourself for my stupidity. I should have been more careful. Neither one of us figured this old piece of crap was being used as a drug lab." Tommy chuckled and the sound morphed into a hacking cough. He propped himself onto his elbows and covered his mouth with his hand.

Owen rubbed circles against the middle of his forehead. He had to be missing something, but as hard as he tried, he couldn't figure out this mess. "Would Bill have experience lacing heroin with Fentanyl? Know where to get all this stuff?"

Marie shrugged and frustration clouded her eyes. "I wish I

had more information for you, but the truth is I don't know much about Bill anymore."

Owen brushed a streak of dirt off her cheek with his thumb. "You've given us plenty. But we'll discuss this more later. Right now, we need to get Tommy out of here." He dropped his hand to Tommy's forearm and gripped it tightly. "Can you stand?"

Tommy wrapped his hand over Owen's arm and pushed himself to his feet. A paleness took over his bronze skin, and a sheen of perspiration covered his forehead. "I might get sick."

"If you need to stop, let me know. The hardest part is getting you down the tree. I need to know you can manage that on your own. I can't carry you."

Tommy took a breath and nodded. "I can do it."

"Okay. I'll go down first, you follow. I'll stay right below you in case you need me. Marie, come down after Tommy."

"Got it," Marie said.

"Move carefully, but not too slowly. We need to meet the EMTs as soon as possible."

Tommy may be on his feet, but that could change. Narcan only lasted up to an hour. If they didn't get Tommy in the hands of medical professions before then, there was no telling what would happen.

He gathered up all the false enthusiasm he could. "Let's go."

MARIE TIGHTENED her grip around the straps securing the heavy backpack to her shoulders. Sweat slid down her spine and made her tank top cling to her skin. They might not have been too far from the park right off the river, but the insufferable heat and Tommy's faltering steps had made the hike much longer.

A small clearing opened among the trees, and they followed a narrow trail to a parking lot at the entrance to the park. An ambulance and police cruiser waited there. The sound of cars from the nearby road, hidden by the covering of trees, roared against the stillness of the afternoon.

The black asphalt under her feet was hard as nails compared to the soggy earth. She stayed a few feet behind Owen, who walked with Tommy's arm swung around his neck, helping his brother with each step.

Owen waved his free hand in the air, and a large deputy with a wide-brim hat jogged toward them. The EMT tugged a gurney through the open door at the back of the ambulance and rolled it behind the man.

"How's he doing?" the officer asked, his voice tight and lips pressed in a firm line.

"You can ask me. I'm right here," Tommy said.

Marie fought a smile. Not one complaint had crossed Tommy's lips since he woke. She couldn't help but wonder if her mom would behave so well after being roused from an overdose.

Lead settled in her stomach. With a drug addict as a mother, she'd witnessed more than she should, but at least she'd been spared watching her mom overdose on the one thing she craved more than anything.

A shudder shot through her. Tommy's life was spared because Owen had been so prepared. Her mom's fate would have been worse if Marie'd been forced to deal with it.

The officer stepped into stride on the other side of Tommy and circled his arm around Tommy's waist. "Fine. How are you?"

"Dizzy, nauseous, my head is pounding, but I'm alive thanks to Owen."

"Owen should have been the one checking that old blind. And why didn't you call me? I had to hear everything from the emergency dispatcher." The older man aimed narrowed eyes and a tight jaw over Tommy's head and straight at Owen.

"I handled it," Owen said, a hard edge to his voice. "I would have called once I got Tommy here."

Another emergency responder had emerged from the front of the ambulance, joining the other paramedic and rushing toward them with the white-sheet covered gurney.

Owen pivoted so he stood in front of the bed and lowered Tommy.

Rivers of sweat poured down Tommy's pale face, and he winced as he sank onto his back.

Fear bit into her heart. Tommy's positive veneer hadn't slipped once while they'd walked, and Marie had stayed behind the two men. She hadn't seen the pain etched on his face or the worry shadowing Owen's eyes.

The deputy grabbed Tommy's hand but stared at Owen as they all hurried toward the waiting ambulance. "I'm going with him. I brought your car. I printed out a bunch of information. The guy—or boy—who drove Bill is Edward Jones. Eighteen years old. Lives with his mother, but she hasn't seen him in weeks. Kid's dad died earlier this year, and he's taken it hard. Mom says he's spiraling out of control, won't go to school. She doesn't know what to do."

Marie's stomach muscles tightened. Eighteen years old? So young and already threw his life away. Anger simmered in her veins. Bill managed to find someone young and vulnerable and turned him into a felon.

Owen and the officer helped the EMTs hoist Tommy into the back of the ambulance. Owen glanced over his shoulder. "Does that name sound familiar?"

She shook her head. "No. But we should doublecheck the notebook I gave you. I might have written down something and can't recall at the moment."

The deputy turned to look at her and widened his eyes. "I'm sorry. Who are you?"

Owen cleared his throat, swinging the other man's gaze his

way. "This is Marie Robinson. The woman who was involved with Bill Flanders. Marie, this is my dad. Sherriff Mike Wells."

Mike nodded and extended an arm.

Marie accepted his outstretched hand and tried to quell the disappointment blooming in her chest. Owen's words were true, but was that all he saw when he looked at her—the woman who was stupid enough to get mixed up with Bill?

She dropped her hand and smoothed her dirt-smeared tank top. What Owen thought of her didn't matter. He was investigating her blood-sucking ex, and she was a victim who would run back home as soon as Bill was found. "Hello. Nice to meet you."

"You, too." Mike dropped her hand and trained his focus back on Owen. "Something else of interest—Edward Jones is Steven Piper's nephew. I put more pressure on the administrative assistant at Piper Properties to get us in touch with him. If he's involved in this mess, there's no telling where those two might be holed up. He has properties all over the county."

Marie's mind wandered to the destroyed lab they'd found in the treehouse. The broken glass and knocked-over equipment told of a hasty escape. They might not have taken all of their stuff, but they'd definitely taken whatever drugs they'd mixed. "Would this kid know how to make a synthetic opioid? I could be wrong, but I think that'd be outside of Bill's capabilities."

Owen glanced at Mike, who shrugged. "Not sure."

One EMT ran to the front of the truck and the other clamped a hand on Mike's shoulder. "We gotta go."

"Go with Tommy. I've got this," Owen said.

Mike pulled Owen into a quick hug, handed him a set of keys, then hopped into the back of the ambulance. "Be careful. Call if you need me."

"Try not to flirt with those nurses," Owen called to Tommy before they slammed the doors closed.

Marie stood beside Owen, the warmth of his body seeping

into her skin, and watched the flashing lights disappear from the parking lot. Owen relaxed against her, and she stood tall to support his weight. "Are you okay?"

Owen sighed and straightened, running his hand over his face. "I will be. I haven't been that scared in a long time. But I can't dwell on it now. I need to look at the information my dad found about Edward Jones and call his mom."

Marie stayed close to his side as they crossed the deserted parking lot to his car. "It doesn't sound like your dad got much from her."

"True, but I need to start somewhere. I don't know anything else about the kid except who his uncle is, and Steven Piper isn't making himself available right now."

"Your dad said he hasn't been going to school. He must be a senior if he's eighteen. Why don't we talk to some of his teachers? Could you talk to his principal? They always seem to know what's going on with kids. Especially in small towns."

Owen turned toward her with a wide grin, some of the haunted shadows slipping from his eyes. "You're brilliant."

She smiled and a different kind of warmth spread through her—one that didn't have anything to do with the temperature.

11

M arie glanced around the neat-as-a-pin car as Owen maneuvered out of the parking lot and headed toward town. Not as much as a straw wrapper littered the floor. She swallowed past the lump in her throat. It'd been years since nervousness had swept through her while alone with a handsome man—and even longer since she'd worried about what a man thought of her.

She yearned to flip down the visor and check the mirror, but she'd probably cringe at her make-up free face and air-dried hair. Why hadn't she swiped some mascara over her lashes or dabbed concealer on the bags under her eyes?

A curve in the road took them over a bridge, separating the river from a man-made lake. Lily pads dotted the surface of the water. She tilted her head and studied the water, the high level nearly brushing against the bottom of the bridge. She swallowed hard, and her heart beat like a heavy drum against her chest. "Is the lake usually so high?"

"No. Water's high all over town with the rain we've gotten. If it doesn't stop soon, it's going to be a nuisance."

Memories of another lake, another life-or-death situation

where control was ripped from her grasp, assaulted her. Goose-bumps erupted on her arms as if the cold water from long ago still clung to her skin.

Marie leaned her temple against the cool glass of the window and glanced up, needing to take her mind far away from the deep, dark abyss beside her. "No rain yet today. That's a good sign."

"The clouds over the horizon don't look good, and the weatherman calls for more rain tomorrow. We'll need to prepare for flooding soon."

She didn't want to think about flooding, about rushing currents hurtling toward her with nowhere to run. She tore her gaze from the passing sky and studied the strong lines of Owen's profile. "You mean in all your spare time?"

Owen snorted and shot her a tight-lipped expression.

She squirmed, fear tingling in her stomach at the impending storm, then turned her gaze back out the window. Brick warehouses and colorful rows of houses dotted either side of the road.

"I have your notebook in the backseat. Do you want to see if anything jogs your memory? We can try to put some pieces together while I drive." Owen slid his left hand to the top of the wheel and stretched his arm over the seat behind him.

"I'll get the notebook." She swiveled toward the back, scooped up the journal she'd kept close to her side for months, and flipped it open.

"I only glimpsed through it but looks like you were pretty thorough." Owen made a left turn toward a part of town she'd never been.

"I tried. Once Nora was born, I devoted myself to two things. Being the best mom I could be, and doing whatever I could to stop Bill from ruining our lives." She scanned the first page, searching for the name Edward Jones or anything that sparked her interest. Each page listed dates, times, and names. She made notes detailing if the name represented someone who'd been to their house or was just brought up in conversation. "The name Eddy is in here. I wonder if that's the same person."

Owen shrugged. "Maybe. We'll find out in a minute."

A large building came into view with a sea of cars in the parking lot. Owen drove to the front of the school and parked beside the sidewalk. Teenagers swarmed out the double doors, backpacks bouncing on their shoulders and cell phones pressed against their ears. "Looks like school just let out."

She noted the worry lines etched around the corners of his eyes. Unable to stop herself, she rested a hand on his forearm. "Are you sure you're okay?" She'd debated asking the question, but he'd shown her compassion and kindness. Asking for his wellbeing was the least she could do.

His gaze dropped to her hand then he locked his eyes with hers. A hint of a smile poked through, turning her insides to mush. "I will be, so will Tommy. But I can't stop and think too much about that. Not right now. But thanks. It's nice to have someone care."

His gratitude made her core tingle and she forced herself to stop touching him and focused on the flood of students hurrying to their vehicles. "Might be easier to talk to the principal without a bunch of kids around." Marie hopped out of the car and studied the young faces of the students who flowed past.

Owen shut off the engine and joined her on the sidewalk. "When I called, the secretary told me the principal would be here until five." He hustled toward the doors with the school logo etched in the glass and opened it wide.

Students rushed out, casting him curious glances before returning their focus to their friends or phones or whatever else needed their attention.

Longing tightened Marie's chest. Renee would be getting out of school for the day. Would she head to the diner to work an evening shift? Or stay home to study? She missed her sister fiercely. Renee deserved the carefree, typical teenage issues most of these kids had. Instead, she was holding down the fort and helping keep their mom clean.

Stepping into the wide hallway, Marie followed Owen to the first door on the right. He ushered her inside the office.

A woman with long gray hair and a welcoming smile sat at a large desk. Stacks of piled-high paper littered the counter behind her and square cubbies lined the wall. She glanced at them with raised brows, but her smile never faltered. "Can I help you?"

Owen held up his identification. "I'm Deputy Wells. I believe we spoke earlier. I need to see Ms. Teller."

Her wide smile failed. "Oh, yes. One second." Grabbing the telephone receiver, she squeezed it between her ear and shoulder and pressed a few buttons. "Patricia, the deputy is here to see you." She nodded and hung up the phone. "Go on back. Her office is the first door on the left."

"Thank you," Owen said.

Marie shot her a timid smile then followed Owen past her desk and down the carpet-lined hall.

The door to Ms. Teller's office stood wide open. Owen knocked on the door frame before entering. A middle-aged woman with shoulder length chestnut hair rose and hurried to offer them a handshake. "Please, come in and close the door. I'm not sure what I can do for you today, but I'll help in any way I can."

Two cushioned chairs with metal armrests sat in front of the desk, and Marie took a seat. She folded her hands in her lap and stared around the room. The blinds on the lone window blocked out the late afternoon sunlight and books lined a tall shelf in the corner. Educational certificates hung on the wall, but no personal effects were in sight.

"I'm Deputy Wells and this is Marie Robinson. Thank you

for making time for us." He took the other seat and cleared his throat. "I need to speak with you about one of your students— Edward Jones."

A frown tugged down her lips. "Has something happened?"

"Edward's name has come out in the course of an investigation. I understand his father passed away recently and his mother is having difficulties with him. I hoped you could shed some light. Friends he spends time with, hobbies or extracurricular activities he's involved in. Anything that could point us to where we could find him."

Ms. Teller blew out a long breath and shook her head. "I hate to say I'm not surprised. He's had a tough time. A lot of the staff have reached out and tried to help him through it, but nothing has worked." She grabbed a pencil and sheet of paper. "Here are the names and information of the parents of a couple of boys Eddy was close to before his dad got sick. They might know something."

Marie's ears perked up. "Does he usually go by Eddy?"

"Yes." Ms. Tell shifted her tired eyes toward Marie. "I don't think anyone ever calls him Edward."

"One more question," Owen said. "You mentioned members of the staff trying to help. Is there anyone who was more successful? Someone who might be able to help find him?"

Ms. Teller leaned back in her chair and sighed, clasping her hands in her lap. "The chemistry teacher, Mr. Silas, seemed to get through to him, but unfortunately he's not here today."

"Will he be here tomorrow? Can I get his contact information?"

Ms. Teller twisted her lips to the side and darted her gaze to the closed door than back to Owen. Tears misted in her eyes, and she cleared her throat. "I'm not sure when he'll be back. His girlfriend was found dead this morning. He'll be needing some time off."

Marie stifled a gasp and fought not to let her jaw drop. Water's Edge was a small town. The chances of two women being found dead this morning were slim. Unless the teacher's girlfriend was from a different town. The tightening of Owen's jaw and his hard gaze told her his thinking lined up with hers.

"I'm sorry for his loss," Owen said slowly. "Do you happen to know what his girlfriend's name was?"

Ms. Teller locked her gaze on Owen. "Erica. Erica Zyler."

ADRENALINE ZIPPED through Owen's veins as he and Marie followed Ms. Teller down the empty hall. Maroon lockers sat snuggly against the walls on both sides, only interrupted when a door to a classroom emerged. Mr. Silas might not be here, but Owen still wanted to look at the chemistry room. He needed to see what kind of equipment the school provided the students for the experiments they did in class.

Ms. Teller opened a door and ushered them inside. Two-person lab benches clogged the room, backless stools tucked under them. Microscopes, textbooks, and Bunsen burners sat neatly on the back wall.

Owen crossed the room and grabbed one of the Bunsen burners. It looked identical to the one he'd seen in the blind, but they all looked the same to him. He whirled around, clasping it in his hand. "Where do you buy your lab equipment?"

A balding man with a white beard and thick glasses rose from behind the small wooden desk at the front of the room. "Can I help you with something, Ms. Teller?"

Ms. Teller stood with her back as straight as the brown hair that skimmed the top of her shoulders. "This is Deputy Wells and his friend. They are here asking questions about one of our students."

The man ran his thick fingers through his beard. "I'm only a substitute, and a new one at that. I don't know how much help I'd be."

Ms. Teller offered him a small smile. "It's okay, Doug. Deputy Wells wanted to see the chemistry lab even though Mr. Silas is out." She faced Owen once more. "If you have any more questions before you leave, please stop by my office. I'm afraid I have an appointment to meet a parent. Take as much time in here as you need."

Doug hurried to them as Ms. Teller left the room.

Marie shifted beside Owen and peered at the burner. She turned a brilliant smile to the old man. Damn if Owen didn't wish she'd flash a smile like that at him "Have you had any equipment missing lately?" she asked.

Doug shrugged. "I couldn't say. This is my first time subbing for Mr. Silas this year. I was a history teacher, so I don't have much experience with this stuff." He flicked his wrist toward the long piece of metal and tubing in Owen's hand. "You could check the storage closet. Not sure if that would give you any answers or not." He hooked a thumb over his shoulder at a wide door in a front corner of the room.

Owen weaved between the lab tables and opened the door. Shelves sat in a U-shape along the interior of the walk-in closet. Cardboard boxes occupied every inch of the space inside. Black marker identified each box. He handed the Bunsen burner to Marie then lifted the crisscrossed top of the box in front of him. The makeshift label correctly identified the textbooks inside, and he wasn't surprised to find the correct contents of the next three boxes.

"This will take forever," Marie said from over his shoulder. "And even if you don't find what he has labeled outside the box, we won't know the reason why. Let's talk to Ms. Teller again. Maybe she has a list of supplies or order forms or something. Maybe there's a discrepancy in the budget or a record of missing equipment. There'd have to be a paper trail if this guy stole from the school."

Owen shook his head and gave the stockpile of crap one last look. "You're right. They have to keep records of everything." He dipped his chin toward Doug. "Thanks."

He pressed the tips of his fingers to the small of Marie's back and led her from the room. He wanted to keep his hand on her back, her skin, hell anywhere she'd let him, but he couldn't think of an excuse to touch her once they stepped back in the empty hall.

He jammed his hands in his pockets. Every minute he spent with Marie revealed something else he liked about her. She was a caring mother and a knock-out, but she was smart, too. Always thinking, always jumping in to give her thoughts and show him a different path to take.

His boots squeaked against the recently buffed floor, and he tightened his jaw. The path he wanted to take with Marie was one he couldn't dare go down.

"Do you think the chemistry teacher is behind all of this?" Marie asked, her voice breaking into his thoughts.

"Maybe. It seems pretty coincidental he has a connection to Eddy and Erica. Not to mention a working knowledge on combining chemicals and access to lab equipment. I need to find this guy and talk to him."

Beep, beep, beep.

The faint sound of a car alarm echoed through the hall, and apprehension tickled the base of Owen's neck. He reached for Marie and pulled her toward the front doors at a clip, hoping his gut was wrong.

They burst onto the now empty sidewalk, into the cool and misty air. Gray clouds had replaced the white, and the lot was nearly empty save a few sedans in the faculty spots.

His cruiser sat at the curb, lights flashing, horn honking.

A spiderweb of splintering glass engulfed his windshield.

12

Owen sat on the edge of the sidewalk and watched the flatbed tow truck haul away his car. On closer inspection, his windshield wasn't the only thing vandalized. Slits punctured two tires, and key marks scratched lines into the paint. Frustration pounded through his veins.

Marie sat beside him, her shoulder pressed against his and her hand on his knee. Her reassuring touch against the rough material of his pants was the only thing keeping him from losing it.

The *click-clack* of heels ricocheted behind them, and he glanced over his shoulder and into the worried eyes of Ms. Teller. He stood and helped Marie to her feet.

Ms. Teller clasped her fingers in front of her, stroking her thumb against her knuckle over and over again. "I'm sorry, but I checked the video feed from the security cameras. The cameras are pointed toward the parking lot, but not directly in front of the doors."

Owen tunneled his hand through his hair. He couldn't catch a break.

"Do you think it was Bill? That he's still following me?" Marie's small voice relaxed the tension coiling around his body.

Ms. Teller bounced her gaze between them. "Who's Bill? I thought you were looking for Eddy?"

Owen wrapped an arm around Marie's trembling shoulders and grazed his fingertips against the skin on her biceps but focused on Ms. Teller. The principal had been helpful and supplied the budget report and inventory list for the chemistry department, but he wouldn't give the woman more information than needed.

"There are many parts to this investigation. Unfortunately, I can't discuss them all with you, but thank you for your help." He fished a business card from his back pocket and handed it to her. "Call me if you have any more information regarding Eddy."

A black SUV barreled into the parking lot and glided to the curb in front of them. The passenger side window slid down, and Katherine stared out from behind the steering wheel. "I hear you might need a ride."

Owen opened the back door for Marie then hopped into the front seat. "Thanks. You remember, Marie, right?"

Katherine flicked her eyes to the rearview mirror and offered a tight smile. "Hello, again."

"Hello."

"Who called you?" Owen asked. The day had been one disaster after another, and the only calls he'd put in were to the sheriff's department and the tow company. Dad was at the hospital with Tommy, and he'd assumed Katherine was still with Pappy.

"Dad. I offered to come get you." She pulled away from the school and onto the main road.

"What about Pappy? He shouldn't be alone." The throbbing in the middle of his forehead took up a steady beat and exhaustion made his eyes heavy. He had so many balls to juggle, and one wrong move would cause everything to come crashing at his feet.

"I'm glad to hear you say that. I got him home in one piece, but he needs someone with him for the next few days. He's weak and shaky on his feet. I was with him all day and need to get some stuff done, and Tommy's being kept overnight for observation. That leaves you." She spared him a quick glance before returning her focus to the road.

Leaning his head against the seat, he sighed and squeezed his eyes shut for a second. The motion of the car through the slow limits relaxed his muscles. "I have too much to do. I can't just sit around babysitting the old man."

"And I can?" Katherine asked, her voice tight and dripping with insult.

He leaned his elbow on the side of the door, just below the rolled-up window, and cradled his head in his hand. "You know that's not what I meant. But I got another lead, and I still need to go through Erica Zyler's space. I can't just let these guys run around town while I twiddle my thumbs at Pappy's. They're dangerous."

"When's the last time you ate? How long have you been awake?" Katherine softened her tone.

As if on command, his stomach growled. "It's been a long day."

Katherine tipped her head behind her and lowered her voice. "What about her? You're dragging her all over, under-standably, but she needs a break...and so do you. We both know cases like this can drag on a lot longer than we'd like. You'll get run down if you don't take care of yourself."

Owen glanced behind him. Marie sat with her head rested against the door, her eyes closed. Katherine was right. He could force himself to go a few more hours, but not Marie. She'd had a day from hell. He needed to take care of her. Needed to get her back to the shelter and Nora. "Fine. I can make some calls and still get some stuff done. But I'll need to take Marie back to Pine Valley first."

"Fine," she mimicked. "I can stay with Pappy a while longer, and you can use my car. I'll come back in the morning. I've shuffled some appointments around to make it work, but I'll need you to stay tomorrow night if possible." A beat of silence passed. "Pappy's been asking about Marie."

He chanced another peek at Marie. Her chest rose slowly, her mouth parted and a softness he hadn't witnessed took over her face. In sleep she could escape the horrors of her life, leaving a peaceful glow that had him fighting the urge to trace his fingertips along her jawline and over her plump lips. "I'm still surprised Pappy's taken to her like he has. He barely tolerates us."

Katherine snorted. "He loves us in his own way. It's just different since Mom died. A large part of him died with her, and what's left of him is haunted by the past. He told me Marie reminds him of Mom. Probably why he's so protective of her."

Owen squinted and studied the dark hair and high cheekbones, a jab of guilt punching him at studying her while asleep. "She doesn't look anything like Mom."

Katherine chuckled. "I think it has more to do with her personality, her situation. He couldn't save Mom, and Marie is his second chance at keeping someone alive."

Marie's eyes fluttered open and locked on his.

Warmth engulfed him, and he winced. She'd caught him staring. He tensed, waiting for a disapproving look or heated words, but a slow smile crept onto her face. He matched her grin with one of his own. "Are you hungry?"

She yawned and rubbed her eyes. "Starving."

"How about we pick up a pizza on our way back to the shelter after Katherine drops us off?" he asked, hoping to grab some more time with her before being forced to leave her side.

She straightened. "What about talking to the chemistry teacher?"

He took a quick glance at the clock and cringed. His day had started before the sun had rose. "I've been working for eleven hours. It's time to take a little break. All our problems will still be there tomorrow. Besides, that baby of yours is probably really missing her mama."

She relaxed into her seat. "I miss her, too It's like I've been missing an arm all day."

Owen faced the front and watched the first drops of rain trickle down from the sky. If the rain didn't stop soon, he'd have one more problem to add to all the rest.

A vise squeezed his heart. He had a sneaky suspicion that when this mess was sorted out, his biggest problem would be how to deal with his feelings for Marie and how he'd let her walk away.

THE DANGER of the day combined with Marie's bone-crushing need to see Nora kept her focus out the window as Owen drove her back to Safe Haven Women's Shelter. The warm pizza he'd picked up along the way sat on her lap, the combination of garlic and pepperoni making her mouth water.

Owen parked Katherine's SUV in the driveway and shut off the engine. "I'll carry the food. I texted Mrs. Collins and let her know we were on the way and bringing dinner."

Marie unclasped her seatbelt and winced. The fullness of her breasts reminded her she wasn't the only one who needed fed. The few hours she'd been away from Nora had been the longest she'd gone without feeding her daughter since her birth. She'd left formula with Mrs. Collins in case Nora was hungry while she was away, but that didn't do anything to help the growing ache in Marie's chest.

"I need to check on Nora then I'll meet you in the kitchen." She waited for him to grab the square box from her lap then hopped out of the vehicle and bounded up the steps to the front door.

Her heart almost burst from her body to find Mrs. Collins waiting in the foyer, Nora nestled in her arms. "Hi, there. I figured you'd need to see this precious one as soon as you arrived."

Marie gathered Nora close and pressed her lips to her forehead. "Hey, baby girl. Mommy missed you so much."

"She missed you, too, but she was a perfect angel while you were gone."

Marie beamed with pride. "Thank you for watching her. I'm going to feed her really quick."

"Take your time," Mrs. Collins said as the door opened, and Owen stepped inside.

"I'll be right back," she called over her shoulder and hurried up the stairs. The warmth of Nora's body seeped through her T-shirt. She cuddled Nora close, savoring the feel of her baby in her arms. Words couldn't describe how much she'd missed Nora, but at least her daughter hadn't been in danger. Hadn't been in the room when her father showed up and shot a man.

She'd been safe and warm, enjoying her time with a houseful of women who adored her.

Once in her room, Marie closed the door and settled into the rocking chair. She adjusted her shirt, placed Nora in her favorite eating spot, and melted against the back of the chair as the pressure that had filled her breasts slowly released.

Nora's head moved and silly sounds gurgled from her mouth as she devoured her evening meal.

Tension relaxed the tight muscles in Marie's neck. Any doubt that Nora had been properly taken care of all floated away. Her daughter was happy and stress free. A perfect bundle of joy in a world filled with chaos.

But she wouldn't think about any of that chaos now. Not while looking down at Nora's full cheeks and pert little nose. This was their moment, their time, their experience. She wouldn't let in anything that would take away from it. Like Owen said earlier, it'd all be there waiting for them later.

When Nora turned her head away, Marie lifted her and smoothed her hand over her little back until she burped, then righted her shirt before heading back downstairs. She pushed open the swinging door to the kitchen, and her heart warmed at the scene she stumbled into.

Mrs. Collins sat at the head of the table while Owen bustled around the kitchen—carrying a stack of napkins in one hand and a pitcher of water with the other. The pizza box sat in the middle of the table, the lid wide open to show off the deliciousness inside.

"Have a seat," Owen said, sliding out a chair.

The gesture was so small, so simple yet something so large. She'd never had a man pull out a chair for her.

"Thanks," she mumbled, heat flaming her cheeks.

"Can I, uh, hold the baby while you eat?" Owen cleared his throat, his eyes wide and filled with hesitation, as if unsure if he should even ask the question.

She struggled not to lift her brow in surprise. Bill had never held his own child, only complained about her cries and the money it took to keep her in diapers. He'd never shown an ounce of concern or even mild interest in Nora.

"Are you sure?" She asked. "Might make it harder for you to eat."

He wrinkled his nose. "I already stole a slice. Mrs. Collins is expecting another guest this evening. It'll be better if I'm gone before she gets here."

"Oh," she said, disappointment crushing her windpipe. She

knew Owen would have to leave at some point, but she'd foolishly hoped he'd hang around a little longer. "Then sure. You can hold her."

Owen stood over her and cradled his arms, waiting for her to deposit Nora into the safe crook he'd created.

"Make sure to hold her head. She likes to see your face. She's a very curious girl, aren't you, love?" Once Nora was settled, Marie sat and placed a piece of pizza on her plate.

Owen beamed at Nora. "Hello, little one."

Mrs. Collins chuckled. "She looks even smaller in your arms."

Marie studied the unlikely pair. The giant man with a scruffy beard and broad shoulders holding the tiny baby cuddled in a pink blanket. Her bones melted, and her heart filled with a sudden burst of joy she wished she could hold onto forever.

Nora gurgled and pumped her little arms.

"Oh, really," Owen said, as if understanding what the baby was saying. "You have an interesting way with words."

"I'm afraid once she starts talking, she'll never stop." Marie grinned then took a bite of the still-hot pizza. She closed her eyes on a moan as the gooey cheese and spicy pepperoni slid down her throat. "Heavenly."

"Agreed," Mrs. Collins said. "Nothing tastes better than a meal I didn't have to cook."

Marie laughed and took another bite. "Do you cook all the meals here?"

"Depends," Mrs. Collins said. "Sadie and Laura help a lot, plus there are other volunteers who venture in to lend a hand when possible—some just not in the kitchen. Dr. Simon stops by to offer free medical attention when needed, and a local shop owner—Elsie—manages the donations. Neither are that good with a stove."

"Both have got to be better than me," Owen said. "Most nights I grab take out or end up eating boxed mac and cheese."

"Oh, so you do have some flaws, huh?" Marie smirked.

Owen's dark brows pinched together, and he lowered his face so he spoke directly to Nora. "Can you believe your mommy would say something like that about me?"

Marie barked out a laugh, enjoying the playful banter around the table. It'd been so long since she'd had this kind of comradery. Since she felt so at ease while enjoying a meal.

Mrs. Collins chuckled and rolled her eyes. "Men are such fragile creatures, but I do appreciate the meal, Owen. For now, I need to head upstairs and get another room ready. Marie, I'll be putting the guest and her two children down the hall from you. Let me know if any issues arise, okay?"

"Okay."

Mrs. Collins stood and reached for her plate.

"Don't worry about the dishes," Marie said. "Tidying up the kitchen is the least I can do."

"Free dinner and no cleaning after holding a baby all day. Nothing gets better than that. Owen, send me a text when you leave so I can set the alarm." Mrs. Collins gave a little wave and disappeared through the door to the front of the house.

A comfortable silence settled in the room, and Marie wished this moment never had to end. She picked at the last pepperoni on her pizza, searching for a way to keep Owen around longer.

But what was the point? He had to go see to Lewis, and she was just some woman who was more trouble than she was worth. Especially to him. Better not to get more invested than she already was. Surely only more heartbreak would follow.

Popping the last bit of her meal in her mouth, she stood and carried the dirty plates to the dishwasher. "Thanks. For everything. I can take Nora now so you can get back to your grandfather."

Owen frowned. "Are you sure? I can stay a bit longer."

She forced a tight smile. "We're good."

Owen carried Nora to her and handed her over. He brushed the side of his finger against the baby's cheek. "Goodnight, then."

Sighing, she watched him leave. If life was different, maybe she could throw caution to the wind and see if this attraction to the handsome deputy could turn into something more. But life was what it was, and dreaming about what could be was useless.

"Come on, baby girl. I need a shower and clean clothes, and you need to sleep."

With her heart suddenly heavy, she climbed the stairs and shut her door. She found a pair of pajamas she'd packed for Nora and got her ready for bed, then settled into the rocking chair to rock her most precious gift.

She studied Nora's heavy eyelids as she struggled to stay awake. "I love you, little one. More than anything in the whole world."

A tiny smile curved Nora's lips and she drifted to sleep seconds before the security alarm blared to life, and fear drove itself into Marie's heart like a knife.

13

Leaving the Safe Haven Women's Shelter was much harder than Owen ever anticipated. He'd wanted Marie to ask him to stay, to linger over the table and find new things to discuss other than the investigation.

He wanted to know her.

Instead, he was driving home alone with the memory of Marie's face etched in his mind and the feel of her baby still in his arms.

He slapped the heel of his hand on the top of the steering wheel. Enough! He had a job to do, and he needed all of his focus on finding a killer.

Swinging onto the town square of Pine Valley, he gave himself a mental kick in the ass. From now on, he'd maintain a professional distance with Marie and her child. Hell, he may not even spend any more time with her after tonight. He'd taken her statement and, she'd given him all the information she had.

Shit.

He'd forgotten to ask if he could hang on to her notebook.

His nerve endings sizzled. Now he had an excuse to call and check on her in the morning, to swing by and see her.

He rolled his eyes. So much for being professional.

His phone rang through the speakers of the vehicle, interrupting his thoughts. He pressed the answer button on the touch screen. "Deputy Wells."

"Owen, it's Marie. Something's wrong." Her panic came through loud and clear, competing with the blaring of an alarm.

A steely calm slipped over his initial burst of fear. "What happened?"

"I came upstairs with Nora, and the security alarm went off. I think someone's trying to break in."

"Where's Mrs. Collins?"

"I...I don't know. Should I try to find her?"

"No. Stay in your room and make sure your door's locked. The local police should be on their way. Do not come out. I'm coming."

"Owen, I'm scared."

The tremor in her voice split his chest in two, and he found a spot to turn around and head straight back to the shelter. "You can keep the line open. I'm right here, okay? You're going to be all right."

"What if it's Bill? What if he found me again?"

He pressed the gas pedal to the floor, blowing over the residential speed limit. He gripped the wheel and squeezed tight until his knuckles threatened to burst through the skin. If Bill hurt one more hair on Marie's head, he'd make the asshole pay.

"He won't get to you or Nora. I promise." He prayed that was a promise he could keep.

He took the corner and sped toward the sound of sirens. Red and blue lights slashed across the darkening sky. "I'm here. You're safe." He pulled behind the police car and slammed on the brakes, shutting of the engine before jumping out of Katherine's SUV.

The blaring alarm shut off, and he leapt up the porch steps. A Pine Valley police officer stood in the foyer and spoke with a concerned Mrs. Collins—a shotgun in her steady hand.

"Oh, Owen. Thank goodness you're here. Marie has to be a mess. I haven't checked on her. I rushed down to make sure no one had gotten in the house."

"She called when the alarm went off." He turned to the tall officer with the shoulder-length hair and bushy beard. He tipped his chin in greeting. "Lincoln. Find anything?"

"Haven't had a chance to check the perimeter, but no signs of forced entry. No one here when I arrived. I want to check around the house. See if anything stands out, or if the alarm was triggered by something else."

Mrs. Collins frowned, fury in her eyes. "You boys know this security system is the best money can buy. Your wife helped me pick it out, Lincoln. The only way that alarm would have gone off is because someone was trying to get inside."

Owen rubbed the back of his neck as the truth of her statement sank in the pit of his stomach like a boulder. Lincoln's wife, Brooke Mather, was a former police officer who ran Crossroads Mountain Retreat—a local rehabilitation center for law enforcement and veterans. If there was one person he'd trust to outfit a home with the best security system possible, it was Brooke.

"I need to take a closer look, and I'll let you know what I find," Lincoln said.

"I'm coming with you," Mrs. Collins said. "No way I'm going to stand around not doing everything I can to protect this home and the people inside it."

He couldn't help but grin at the feisty old woman. She'd proven herself in the past as one hell of a protector.

"Do you mind if I check on Marie?"

"Go, go! Second floor. She's the first door on the right."

He took the steps two at a time and jogged to her room. He knocked gently. "Marie. It's Owen. Everything's okay."

The door inched open, only a tiny sliver of her face visible in the crack. "Are you sure? Was it Bill?"

"I'm not sure what triggered the alarm, but Officer Sawyer and Mrs. Collins are checking about that now. If Bill was here, he's not anymore."

Marie flung the door open and launched herself into his arms. Her whole body trembled. Tears leaked from her eyes and soaked through his shirt. "I hate this. I hate not knowing where Bill is and when he's going to pop up. I never feel safe. Can never let my guard down."

He held her close, smoothing a palm against the small of her back over and over again. She felt so good in his arms—felt so right. "I'm sorry. I'll find him. I swear to you."

She pulled back, her face so close to his. The tip of her nose was red. Her eyes puffy and wide. "I don't even care about me. But what if he gets Nora? What if he takes her from me or hurts her? I couldn't live with myself if anything happened to her."

The agony in her face twisted his gut. Unable to stop himself, he flattened a palm against her jawline and Lord help him if she didn't lean into his touch. "I will protect Nora with my life. Do you understand me? I'll protect both of you."

"How?" she asked.

Before he could answer, heavy footsteps pounding up the stairs turned them both toward the curving stairwell. He dropped his hand from the soft skin on her face but kept one arm firmly around her shoulders.

Lincoln stopped at the top of the steps. "You're both going to want to see something."

"Give us a second," he said, then peered over Marie's head into her room. "Where's Nora?"

"In the portable crib. Still fast asleep, the little angel."

"Is it okay if I pick her up? I don't want to leave her or you in here alone." He didn't want to wake the baby, but he wanted to keep her and Marie in his sight.

One side of Marie's mouth ticked up. "If she wakes, she wakes. But I can grab her."

He stepped around her to the little nylon crib beside the bed. "Sounds weird, but I missed the little booger." Bending over, he scooped up Nora and held her close.

Her little body jerked a bit and her arms stretched over her head. Green eyes blinked open, and he swore she smiled up at him before dozing back to dreamland.

His heart tripled in size.

"Ready?" Marie asked, stealing his attention.

He nodded then led the way downstairs. He took each step extra careful, not wanting to trip or do anything that could hurt Nora.

Mrs. Collins and Lincoln stood in the foyer.

Lincoln held an evidence bag in his hand. "I found this. Smashed through one of the windows at the back of the house."

"Is that a brick?" Marie asked, squinting as if to decipher exactly what was in the bag.

Owen leaned forward, and his blood transformed to molten lava. "Does that say 'See you soon'?"

Lincoln nodded.

Marie took a step back and lifted a trembling hand to her mouth. "He found me. Again. I can't stay here."

Mrs. Collins grabbed Marie's hand. "Don't be silly. We're equipped to deal with all kinds of threats."

"I'm sure you are, but this is bigger than me." Marie shook her head. "I can't bring danger to the doorstep of a place that's supposed to protect women."

"You can stay with me," Owen said. "You and Nora."

Lincoln's blond brows rose high, but he kept his mouth shut.

Marie stared at him, eyes wide and filled with uncertainty. "Is that a good idea? You have to stay with Lewis, and Bill already found me there. Lewis was hurt because of me."

"No, Pappy was hurt because of Bill. And I wasn't there when that happened. This time, I won't leave your side. Not until Bill's behind bars and you and Nora are both safe."

Marie nodded, her shoulders drooping as if tension was melting away.

He held Nora closer, and a fierce sense of protectiveness swept through him like he'd never known before. This little life depended on her mother, depended on him. And he'd do everything within his power to make sure this baby grew up in a world filled with happiness, a world where dangers weren't lurking around every corner.

A world where her own father could never, ever hurt her.

STEAM SWIRLED around the small bathroom, and Marie used a hand towel to clear the fog from the mirror. After packing up for her and Nora, she'd come back to Lewis' house with Owen and finally gotten to take her shower.

Not like it'd helped much.

Bags hung heavy under her eyes, and her cheeks sank in as if she hadn't eaten in weeks. She'd lost weight the past month but hadn't paid attention to how it affected her body until now. Sighing, she grabbed a comb from her toiletry bag and ran the wide teeth through her wet hair.

Vanity wasn't a luxury she could afford right now, but she couldn't help swiping mascara through her lashes and adding a splash of color to her face before putting on her sleeping tank and shorts and venturing from the bathroom to find Owen and Lewis.

With her belly full and body clean, exhaustion weighed down her every step. The soft orange hues of twilight might be pouring through the window, but she longed to close her eyes and lock away her problems for another day. Unfortunately, that wasn't an option quite yet.

Peering into the darkened family room off the far side of the kitchen, she spotted Lewis in his recliner and Owen on the far side of the love seat, their heads ducked toward each other as they spoke in hushed tones. Nora sat in a little chair that had Mrs. Collins had insisted they take with them, cooing and smiling as if a part of the conversation.

Marie paused in the doorway, not wanting to interrupt the intimate moment between these two men. Two men who days ago were strangers, and now had wormed their way into a part of her soul with their kindness.

She ached to step into the room and be a part of the casual, cozy moment that was so normal for so many people. Not as a victim who needed protected, but one of them—part of a whole picture, a family who showed up for one another no matter the cost. Instead, she was an outsider, uncertainty keeping her at a distance. She didn't belong here...she didn't belong anywhere except a trailer park outside Gatlinburg with a fractured family she did everything in her power to keep together.

"You gonna just stand there all night, girl?" The words were heavy on Lewis' breath, as if each syllable he spoke took far more effort than it should.

Marie smiled and entered the room, taking the spot beside Owen on the love seat. Nora's gaze immediately found her. "I don't want to intrude."

Owen looked at her with tented brows. "You're never an intrusion. Pappy and I were just going over some things."

Lewis clicked his tongue. "Things you don't need to be concerned about. We'll get this all sorted out, and you can get back to your life."

Gratitude swept through her, making her limbs tingle. She'd never had people so concerned about her—constantly trying to keep her and her daughter safe—but she was in this all the way. "I appreciate you looking out for me, but I'd like to hear what you've learned." She shot Lewis a warm smile, hoping her words wouldn't upset him.

Lewis grumbled and reclined back in his chair, flicking his hand toward Owen. "Go ahead then, tell her."

Owen turned toward her, and his knee brushed against hers. "My dad called to give an update on Tommy. He'll be released in the morning and is surprisingly ready to go back to work. While at the hospital, Dad called Erica's boss. He and Tommy will head to her office tomorrow to check out her work computer and files. But her boss mentioned she used to work more from her home. I need to head over there in the morning and see if I can find a personal computer she used for work."

Marie nodded. "All right. What about Mr. Silas? Have you tried to contact him? Maybe we can talk to him when we're done at Erica's."

Owen shifted his gaze to his grandpa then back to her. "It might be better for you to stay at the house. Katherine will be here all day, and she's more than capable of keeping you and Nora safe."

Marie trembled and wrapped her arms around herself. "No. I don't know her. I don't trust her like I do you. Nora and I will stay out of your way, I promise. But please, take us with you." She hated the whine in her voice, but she couldn't stop the panic from infusing so much emotion into her words. Owen had become her safe place, her rock, and as much as her growing feelings scared her, the idea of being without him while Bill was out there scared her more.

Owen squeezed her shoulder, letting his palm rest against her. How could one simple touch from a man she barely knew loosen the knot of anxiety in her gut? "I don't know where the day will take me, and I don't want you or Nora in danger. You'll be safer here."

She dropped her chin, keeping her gaze on the red polish on her toenails. Stupid tears welled up in her throat. Why would he want her help? She had no education, no experience. She was nobody.

"Would you look at me?"

When she refused, he lifted her chin with his thumb. She blinked, trying to keep the moisture that threatened to spill over from her eyes.

"I want you to be safe. Period. You've been a huge help today. In so many ways. If you'd rather come with me tomorrow, I'd love it. But if you feel uncomfortable or threatened and want to come back here, just say the word. You and Nora come first."

"Okay," she whispered, her heart pounding faster than the swirl of the ceiling fan above her.

"Good," Lewis mumbled. "I don't need two women fussing over me all damn day. At least one of you will be out of my hair."

Marie rose to her feet, crossed the room to Lewis' side, and grinned. "The last place I want to be is out of your hair. I'm glad you're okay."

Lewis lifted the side of his mouth in a half-smile and placed an old, weathered hand on hers. "Back at ya, girl. Now get some rest. Who knows where that grandson of mine will drag you off to?"

Bidding them both a goodnight, she scooped up Nora and escaped to the spare room with a delicious image of exactly where she'd like Owen to drag her. After settling Nora and resting her in the portable crib, she slipped between the cool cotton sheets. Her eyes drifted shut and a smile lifted her lips. Her life might be a world class disaster, but Owen waited in her dreams to whisk her off her feet and kiss away every bit of fear that clung to her.

If only her dreams stood a chance at becoming reality.

14

The next morning, Marie stepped out of Owen's new cruiser onto the side of the road. Water splashed up her bare calf as she unbuckled Nora from her car seat in the back of Owen's new cruiser and settled her into the wrap on her chest. Street parking was the only option in the old section of the city. Well, besides the narrow gravel driveway that was already occupied.

A chill swept over her, and she covered a blanket over Nora's head. The assault of heavy rain had dropped the temperature, and she wished she'd grabbed a hoodie when they'd left the house after breakfast. Owen hurried to her side, and they ran across the small patch of grass to the old Victorian house that had been converted into two apartments—one resident on top and one on the bottom.

Erica Zyler had resided in the bottom apartment.

Marie followed Owen to the narrow porch at the front of the house. Water dripped from the ends of her hair. She rubbed her hands up and down Nora's back. The sound of cars behind her whooshing through the soon-to-be-flooded street worked her nerves as Owen unlocked the door.

"How do you get to the upstairs apartment?" she asked, glancing around.

"There's a staircase around back. I bet it leads to another door that goes into the house. I'm not sure how long the house has been a duplex, but the owner would have had to renovate to make it work." Owen tipped his head toward a metal box on the far end of the porch, protected from the elements inside a screened enclosure. "Like that. Normally a fuse box would be in a basement, but I'm guessing the landlord needed to access it without going into either apartment, so he had an electrician wire it out here."

Marie spared another glance over her shoulder at the metal box, and then stepped through the door as soon as Owen disarmed the alarm and swung it open.

Heavy rain splattered against the window of the living room. Thunder boomed and shook the glass, causing the lights Owen had just turned on to flicker. Marie slipped off her saturated flip-flops and stepped further into the empty apartment.

Soft carpet cushioned her feet, and she curled her toes against the cozy material. She studied the room. Framed pictures of laughing women and mismatched knick-knacks like elegant candlestick holders beside a ceramic unicorn showed a resident with a fun sense of humor who spent time choosing the things she placed in her personal space. A thick gray blanket hung over the edge of the cream-colored sofa. Pink running shoes lay scattered by the front door.

A jolt of sadness shook Marie's already trembling legs, and she leaned against the back of a tufted armchair in the corner of the room. Erica Zyler would never curl up under the blanket or run in her favorite pair of tennis shoes again.

"Are you all right?" Owen placed a hand on her shoulder and dipped his chin, the lines on his forehead expressing his concern.

Marie shrugged and held her daughter close. "Being in her apartment and knowing she'll never come home is sad."

Another crash of thunder rumbled through the apartment, and a flash of lightning sparked outside the window. Marie jumped and rubbed a hand over Nora's back.

Owen squeezed her shoulder, moving his fingers against the tight muscles in her neck. "I'm sorry. I didn't think about what it'd be like for you to come here. It is sad, but hopefully we can find something that will bring Erica justice. If you want, you can sit and wait for me to comb through everything."

Marie sucked in a deep breath and gathered as much courage as she could. "I want to help."

Owen nodded and pulled a pair of gloves from a small duffle bag he'd laid at his feet. "I have clearance to be here as the lead investigator, but you should put these on. Try not to move anything. If I see something I need your input on, I'll let you know. Stay close and tell me if anything jumps out at you."

Marie nodded. She wasn't a police officer, so there wasn't much else she could do. Heck, she wasn't sure if she was even supposed to be here, but Owen going off to investigate without her wasn't an option any longer. Not when Bill's whereabouts were a complete unknown and he'd already come after her twice.

"I want to do a quick walk-through first. Chances are what I want is on a computer somewhere, but you never know where else people might put something...or what else might be helpful in tracking Bill."

Marie followed behind Owen as he went from room to room, checking stacks of papers and glancing between pages of books. She swept her gaze along every cluttered surface they encountered—the kitchen table, the bathroom counter, the nightstand in the bedroom. Erica left evidence of a woman who led a full life, as well as a messy one. No dust or dirt lingered around the space, but Erica clearly wasn't one who believed everything had a proper place.

Once Owen surveyed the apartment, he circled back to the small bedroom at the end of the hallway. The apartment didn't boast of a designated office space, but a sleek laptop buzzed on an antique desk tucked between the side of the unmade bed and the wall.

Marie fought the urge to pull back the light blue duvet and fluff the eyelet lace-covered pillows. Instead, she stood behind Owen as he perched on the edge of the bed and lifted the top of the laptop.

Uneasiness settled into the pit of Marie's stomach, and she focused on the water trailing down the outside of the uncovered window as rain poured down in droves. Diving into all parts of Erica's life was necessary, but it was still invading another woman's privacy.

A boom of thunder collided with the thoughts whirling in her brain, eliciting a small cry from Nora. The electricity flickered again, leaving only the natural light of a sunless day for a handful of seconds before washing them in light once more.

"Crap," Owen muttered. "I need a password to get to her home screen."

Marie peered over his shoulder. "Did you notice any planners or journals laying around? Sometimes people write down their passwords. Especially at home. Less chance of people finding them."

Owen opened the lone drawer in the center of the desk. "Looks like a ton of receipts. She wasn't much of a bookkeeper."

Marie expelled a sad chuckle. "She wasn't much of a housekeeper either, but I think I would have liked her."

Owen pulled wrinkled slips of paper from the drawer and piled them together after scanning them. "She probably kept these for reimbursement from work or tax purposes. I recognize a lot of these names. Local bars, night clubs, hot spots in some of the rougher areas. I'll need to pour over them closer, but they're all time stamped. I might get lucky and pull footage at some of these places."

Marie turned and studied the rest of the room. If Erica was half as paranoid as her, she wouldn't have kept a journal of any kind where it could be easily found. She rounded the edge of the bed and glanced at the top of the nightstand. A pile of books and a reading lamp covered the surface, and no drawers offered more storage underneath even though the thick wooden top should have enough room to hold a few items inside. She fisted her hand and knocked on the top...*thwack, thwack*. The hollow noise competed with the constant drizzle against the converted old house.

Owen swiveled toward her. "What was that?"

Marie screwed her lips to the side and studied the wooden table. "It sounds hollow. The wood's been painted, and it's obvious the piece was refurbished. Do you think she could have something inside?"

Owen crouched beside the stand. "Maybe."

He placed the books and lamp on the bed then ran his hand over the wood and along the sides of the stand. He dipped his hand under the gray-painted furniture, and a grin split his face. He twisted the angle of his arm, the motion shaking the sturdy piece of wood. He slid his arm out from beneath the nightstand and stood with a palm-sized pink journal in his hand. "You're a genius."

She lifted her toes and clasped her gloved hands over her mouth, the taste of rubber attacking her lips. She cringed and dropped her hands to her sides. "You might want to see what's written inside before you say that."

Owen flipped open the first page. "Interesting."

"Passwords?"

"Maybe. The first page has a lot of random words and numbers. Some of the letters are jumbled together and don't spell anything. Looks like it could be passwords for different sites." Owen flipped through a few pages and whistled low. "She has names and locations in here that could mean anything. I still want to go through the computer, maybe she has more detailed information, but there's definitely a reason she hid this."

Marie wrapped her arms around Nora's back, hating the chill racing down her spine. "Something she found—something that could be in there—got her killed. I wish she would've done a better job of staying under the radar."

Owen raised his brows and lifted the side of his mouth in a sad smile, but kept his gaze locked on the notebook. "I bet she wishes that, too." He sucked in a breath. "She wrote last week she walked along the river to get a look at Bill's house, and someone shot an arrow at her. Might explain the divots in the trees we found yesterday. I need to call those stores Tommy mentioned about the feather. I might get lucky and tie the materials to someone."

"Can you take the evidence with us and go? This place is depressing." Marie glanced toward the open bedroom door.

"Sure. Let me grab my bag, and I'll gather what I need. Do you want to shut down the computer?"

Marie nodded, and Owen hurried out the door. Averting her gaze from the decorative pillows scattered across the bed and clothes strewn along the floor, Marie made a beeline for the computer. She sat on the edge of the bed and moved the cursor toward the shutdown button on the corner of the screen.

A pulse of thunder beat through the room. The lone light on the center of the ceiling sputtered then died. A squeak escaped her parted lips.

Calm down. It's just a storm that knocked out the power.

She rose on shaky legs, and a glare bouncing off the window caught her attention. Slowly making her way through the dim room, she peered out the window and fear lodged in her throat.

A dark-clothed figure moved between the low foliage crowded beside the house next door, the shadow morphing from a creeping blob to a lurking silhouette who stared directly at her.

OWEN SECURED the journal in his duffel bag then the lights cut out. No surprise the way the electricity had flickered with every rumble of thunder. At least he'd found what he needed.

"Marie?" He shouted. "Everything all right?"

Leaving the bag by the door, he turned toward the bedroom. The dark clouds blanketing the morning sky blocked any natural light from flowing into the apartment.

Hurried footsteps barreled toward him. Marie fumbled from the hallway, her ragged breaths loud without the hum of electricity. "I saw something outside. Someone was hiding in the bushes on the side of the house next door. He looked in the window."

Anxiety ricocheted between his ribs. "Stay here while I check outside. Lock the door behind me." Grabbing the phone from his pocket, he tossed it her way. "Call 911."

Marie snatched the phone from the air and nodded.

Bang!

Owen whipped toward the sound.

"Oh my God," Marie whimpered. "Was that a gun shot?"

"Sounded like it came from the front. Call the police but stay with me." If Bill or someone else was outside with a gun, he didn't want to leave Marie and Nora alone to fend for themselves. But he needed to see if someone needed help.

Marie ran to him, one fist closing around the material of his T-shirt at his back while her other hand stayed glued to Nora.

Her body heat warmed him, but he couldn't think of what her nearness did to his hormones right now.

He grabbed the gun he'd harnessed at his side and crept toward the front door. The soft glow of his phone caught his peripheral visual. A beat passed, the sound of the ringing unusually loud in the quiet space, and Owen closed his hand around the doorknob.

Marie cleared her throat. "I need police assistance at...crap, where are we?"

Owen kicked himself for not making the call and grabbed the phone. "This is Deputy Wells. I'm at 502 Oak Street. Shots fired and possible sighting of fugitive. Backup needed now." He clicked off the line and handed the phone back to Marie. "Keep it just in case. Ready?"

"Yes." Her response came out in a hushed whisper that kissed the back of his neck.

He pushed the door open wide and tightened his grip on the gun, swinging around to face whatever lurked before him.

A large body lay sprawled on the stairs, as if gunned down while he sprang toward the house.

Marie gasped and buried her face against the back of his neck.

Owen scanned the streets, his nerve endings on high alert. He tiptoed toward the body, his muscles tight and tension coiled across his shoulders. Blood pooled beneath the face-down body. Owen crouched to place his fingers at the base of the man's neck. A weak pulse beat against his fingers. "He's alive, but this isn't Bill or Eddy Jones. He's much bigger than either of them. Let me see the phone."

Marie handed him the device.

Standing, he made another call to the authorities. He didn't just need backup; he needed an ambulance.

Crash!

Marie jumped and tightened her shaking arms around his midsection. "What was that?"

"Sounds like glass shattered inside." Indecision tore him in two. Instinct and training screamed at him to investigate the sound and find who was responsible for the injured man at his feet. But he couldn't leave Marie and Nora. "We can't do anything for this guy until the ambulance comes. But if someone just broke in the house, I need to check it out."

Wide, terror-filled eyes stared at him. "It's dangerous."

Owen cupped her cheek with his hand and skimmed the pad of his thumb against her smooth skin. "It could be Bill. I can catch him, and we can put this whole thing behind us. I'll keep you safe. I promise."

Marie's chin trembled and uncertainty skittered across her face, but she nodded.

Owen led her back inside, keeping his gun trained in front of him. If someone crashed through a window, they had limited options. The lone window in the living room was visible as soon as they entered the apartment, the glass still intact. He made his way through the rest of the apartment, clearing each room as they went, until they reached the bedroom.

Marie's tense body stayed glued to him, and he slowly entered the last room left to secure. Cool air rushed through the open door and greeted them.

Adrenaline surged in his blood. "Stay in the hall," he whispered behind him. The intruder wasn't in the rest of the apartment, which meant he could only be in one place.

Swinging around the doorframe, he trained his weapon from one corner of the room to the next. The window was smashed and glass scattered across the floor, bits of the broken window laying on the bed, but no one stood inside.

Owen took two long strides to the closet and searched inside. Nothing. He dropped to the ground and searched under the bed. Empty. He skirted around the bed and studied the broken window. Streaks of mud trailed down the wall from the bottom casing of the window, and blades of soggy grass lingered in the carpet.

Someone had definitely been inside, but why? He turned toward the other side of the bed, and his blood pressure spiked. No one was inside because they'd gotten what they came for.

Erica's laptop was gone.

15

The scent of disinfectant coated the inside of Owen's nostrils. He hated hospitals. Hated the attempt to sterilize the overpowering presence of death and pain and agony. Agony of both the patients and their loved ones, helplessly sitting with their hands folded in their laps and fear in their eyes as they waited to hear whatever news the doctors delivered.

He bit into his cheek and blocked the memories of being the helpless family member waiting to hear what had happened to his mother and receiving the life-changing news that she was dead.

His footsteps echoed off the shiny floors as he hurried toward his brother's room, Marie hustling beside him with Nora snuggled against her. A phone call to his dad earlier confirmed Tommy had yet to be released. Might as well stop by and see how he was doing before heading out. He glanced at the square plaques by the doors with the black numbers and turned into room 112.

Tommy sat on the side of the bed, his feet flat on the floor and wearing his perfectly pressed uniform. He tapped the tip of his shoe against the ground, as if needing to expel energy. Unused medical equipment sat beside the neatly made bed, and a twenty-four-hour news channel dominated the television screen mounted in the corner of the room.

His dad sat in a pale green chair in front of the lone window, his head tilted back to watch the news show.

Owen stepped further into the room and cleared his throat. "I thought you were getting discharged today? Did you two decide to stay put and watch TV instead?"

Tommy twisted to face him and grimaced. "I've been ready for hours. I don't understand why it takes so long for the doctor to just sign the darn paperwork so I can leave."

Mike stood and nodded toward Marie. "Hello, again. Who's your sidekick?"

"This is Nora," she said, shifting to show the baby's face to Mike.

"She's beautiful," he said with a small smile then focused on Owen with raised brows. "Any word on the gunshot victim?"

Owen rubbed a hand over his face. "He made it through surgery, but he's in the Intensive Care Unit and hasn't woken up. The victim was Damon Silas."

Tommy whistled low. "Erica Zyler's boyfriend and the chemistry teacher from the high school?"

Owen nodded. "One and the same. He's the one person who could break this wide open, and I can't even speak to him."

"He's not the only person," Mike said. "I finally connected with Steven Piper. He's in his office all day. Said to stop by and see him when you get the chance, and he'll answer any questions you have."

Marie shifted beside him, running the tip of her finger along the side of Nora's cheek. "Who's Steven Piper?"

"He owns Piper Properties and is responsible for purchasing the property your house sits on." The last few days had whirled by like a tornado. Steven Piper had slipped his mind, and he'd forgotten to ask Marie if the name sounded familiar. "He's been difficult to connect with. Have you heard his name before?"

Marie shook her head and the long wisp of her ponytail swung with the motion.

A soft knock sounded at the door, and a middle-aged woman in blue scrubs entered the room. "Sorry to keep you waiting, Mr. Wells. You know how it is in small hospitals. Too many patients, not enough staff." She handed over a pile of paperwork. "The doctor just signed your discharge papers and you're free to go. We recommend you make a follow-up appointment with your personal care physician."

"No one needs to check him over again before he leaves? What about warning signs for bringing him back?" Mike frowned, worry shining from his large eyes.

Owen clapped a hand on Tommy's shoulder and squeezed. "He'll be fine. He's not the first guy I've known who's needed Narcan. The doctor wouldn't release him if he wasn't ready, and Tommy's a trained officer. He knows the signs of unforeseen issues more than most people."

The nurse smiled at Mike. "Parent's always worry the most, don't they, Sheriff? The paperwork is very thorough and lists any concerns that could arise."

Tommy stood and glanced down at the stack of papers. "Thank you, Beatty. You've all been wonderful, but I'm ready to get out of here."

Beatty laughed, the sound bouncing off the bare walls. "Don't worry, we're ready for you to leave. You all have a nice day." She turned her warm smile at each of them then hurried out the door.

Tommy scooped up a duffel bag from the floor and hoisted it over his shoulder. "All right. Where to next?"

Mike grabbed the nylon strap of the bag and yanked it away from Tommy. "I got this. How about I drive you home? Or even to your grandpa's? You two can keep each other company, and your sister can get some relief."

Tommy tightened his jaw and shook his head. "No way. I've been holed up in this place for the past twenty-four hours doing nothing more than twiddling my thumbs. If the doctor says I'm fine with no restrictions, I'm fine. Let's get to work."

Mike opened his mouth, but Owen cut in before his dad said something else to upset Tommy. "Why don't you two go speak to Erica's boss? We might have lost access to her home computer, but maybe she has information saved at work. I've got a guard posted by Damon's room just in case and will be notified as soon as he's able to speak with me. Maybe I'll get lucky and Steven Piper can give us the information I need to find where Bill's hiding."

Tommy headed for the door, slapping Owen on the back and throwing Marie a wink on the way out of the room. "Perfect. We'll keep you posted if we find anything. Hurry up, Pops. I don't know where you parked, and you're driving."

A low growl emanated from his dad, and Owen tensed his shoulder and waited to take on the brunt of his frustration. Instead, Mike came to a stop beside Marie and dipped his chin to bring her gaze to his. "Keep an eye on my boy. I'm already worried enough about one of them. You're a mom, so I know you understand what it means to worry about your child. Call me if he stops listening to reason."

Marie's lips spread into a shy grin. "I'll look after him."

Mike pressed his lips together, gave her a small nod, then hurried out the door. He lifted his hand in a wave. "I'll be in touch."

Owen stood for a second and let the emotion from his father's words pass through him. He wasn't sure what choked him up more—his father's concern over his wellbeing or the idea of Marie looking out for him.

MARIE SUPPRESSED a shuddering breath as she jogged through the rain to the main office of Piper Properties. She opted to keep Nora snuggled in her car seat with a blanket over the detachable chair. Luckily the small parking lot in front of the stand-alone red brick building was mostly deserted, and Owen parked close to the office. A white awning stretched in front of the door, and she dashed under its protection.

Owen opened the door and took the heavy seat from her. He pressed his firm palm against the small of her back and ushered her inside.

Her stomach churned, both from the excitement of his touch and in protest of the lack of food she'd had since morning. Afternoon had come while they'd lingered in the hospital, but their appointment with Steven Piper was more important than grabbing a bite to eat.

Luckily, she could feed Nora no matter where she was, and her little love had quickly fallen asleep once her belly was full.

Marie pressed a hand against her stomach as Owen approached the pretty young blonde behind the lone desk in the reception area. Pictures of smiling men and women dominated the walls, and a coffee station sat in the corner. The smell of a fresh pot called to her, but the caffeine wouldn't help her jangled nerves.

The woman at the desk glanced up from the computer with a pleasant curve of her lips and questioning eyes. "Hello. May I help you?"

Owen presented the receptionist his badge. "I'm Deputy Wells, and this is Marie Robinson. We're here to speak with Steven Piper. He's expecting us."

She nodded and her brown eyes turned solemn. "One second." She lifted the receiver from the old-fashioned phone and tapped a few numbers on the keypad. "Hi, Steve. The deputy is here to see you." She replaced the receiver. "Go on back."

"Thank you." Owen rounded the desk and started down the short hallway.

Marie stayed a step behind him, her gaze cast on the worn burgundy carpet and unease flowing through her blood stream. Police reports, another gunshot victim, and even more questions consumed her morning. She couldn't handle much more, and after what she'd learned about Eddy Jones, this meeting was bound to bring nothing good to the mix. But hopefully, it could at least bring answers.

A door at the end of the hall swung open and a balding man with thick, black-framed glasses and a deep frown lingered in the doorway.

Owen closed the distance between them and stretched out his hand. "Good afternoon, Mr. Piper. Thank you for seeing us."

"Please, call me Steven." Steven shook Owen's hand then reached for her, squeezing her palm for a beat before turning back into his office. He sat behind a large oak desk, piles of paper stacked high around a flat-screen monitor. He motioned to the two leather bucket chairs in front of the desk with a wave of his hand. "Make yourself comfortable."

Marie sank into the smooth leather. The dampness of the rain clinging to her thighs made the material rub against her skin. She sat with her back ramrod straight and waited for Owen to speak. She was an observer, and she'd prefer to say as little possible and get out of there quickly.

Owen set Nora's carrier between the two chairs then sat beside her. He leaned forward with his forearms resting on his knees, hands clasped together. "I understand you spoke with the sheriff earlier, and he filled you in on our investigation."

Steven sighed and nodded, rubbing a hand over the white stubble that shadowed his chin. "He gave me the bare minimum. I'm afraid I still don't understand what's going on. He said you're searching for Eddy in connection with a murder investigation. I just can't believe he'd do something like that."

The exhaustion in Steven's voice squeezed Marie's heart. She understood all too well the emotions that came along with trying to keep a family member out of trouble—and the overwhelming feeling of failure when that person let you down.

"We believe your nephew is harboring a murder suspect. There are also suspicions that he's involved in the manufacturing and possible distribution of drugs. Do you know where your nephew is hiding? Is there a history of drug use in his family?" Owen asked.

Steven rested an elbow on his desk and cradled his palm around his head. He squeezed his eyes shut for a beat, and tears misted in his blue eyes when he opened them again. "It was really hard on Eddy when my brother-in-law got sick. He was very close to his father, and watching the cancer take away his life little by little made Eddy bitter and very angry. I suspected Eddy stole some of my brother's pain pills, but I was so lost in my own grief I didn't handle it right—didn't know how to handle it. I tried to find ways to keep him busy, make him happy, hoping it would help."

Understanding tightened Marie's chest, and she couldn't keep quiet. "It's almost impossible to help someone who doesn't want to be helped." The words croaked from her dry throat. She'd lived this man's same pain her entire life and wanted to offer whatever she could to ease his conscious.

He gave her a sad half-smile and sniffed back his emotions. "I should have tried harder."

Owen straightened. "What did you do to help? What types of things did you think would make him happy when he was in so much turmoil?"

Steven shrugged. "It might sound dumb, but I bought a small patch of land and had a little house built. Eddy and his dad loved to hunt together. Even when my brother was too weak to hunt with Eddy, he'd still go to the house and watch out the back window, hoping to get a glimpse of the boy doing something he loved." He dropped his forearm to the desk and widened his eyes. "Maybe that's where he is. At the house. I haven't been there in months, but Eddy has a key."

Marie deflated against the back of her chair. If Steven thought Eddy would be at the house she'd lived at with Bill, he didn't have the answers they needed.

"Is this house located on the river, just north of town?" Owen asked.

Steven nodded. "Yes."

Owen shook his head. "We've been to that property, and no one's there. Is there anywhere else he would go? Any friends you know who would let him crash and keep it a secret?"

"I don't know many of his friends."

"What about properties your company's working on? Would he be able to gain access to any of the work sites and hole up for a few days?"

Steven rubbed his temples. "I don't think so. I run a pretty tight ship. But I'll double check. I'll contact all my supervisors right away. Hell, I'll go out to the work sites myself to make sure he's not there. I hate to see him ruin his life by doing something so stupid, but maybe hitting rock bottom is the best thing for him."

Owen stood, hooked the car seat carrier on his forearm, and fished a business card from the back pocket of his jeans. "I appreciate the assistance. If you find him, or anything else comes to mind, please let me know."

Steven took the card and turned it between his fingers.

Marie rose to her feet. She wasn't a cop, but her gut told her this man wasn't involved in any way with Bill or the crimes he'd committed. She offered him a tight smile and followed Owen to the door. A thought entered her mind, and she turned back to the sad older man. "You said Eddy and his dad liked to hunt. Did they hunt with a bow?"

Steven arched his brows and tilted his head to the side. "Sometimes. Depends on the season I suppose."

Owen took a step forward. "Did they use a primitive bow? Make their own arrows?"

Steven chuckled. "No way. My brother-in-law was a wonderful person, but he couldn't build a birdhouse if you cut the wood for him and all he had to do was hammer in a nail."

Disappointment weighed her down. Not only had Steven Piper provided no answers for them, but he left them with one more question—if Eddy Jones wasn't the one shooting on Lewis' land with homemade arrows, then who was?

16

Owen stepped outside and tilted his chin toward the sun peeking through a sea of clouds. If the forecast was right, the warm rays wouldn't stick around for long, but he wanted to enjoy them while he could. "How about a walk? We can head downtown and grab some lunch."

"She might get heavy," Marie said, nodding toward Nora nestled in her carrier. "Do you want me to get her out?"

"Nah, I got her."

Marie hoisted her bag higher on her shoulder then crossed her arms over her middle as she walked beside him. "I never know what to do with my hands when I'm not holding her. It's a weird feeling."

A ridiculous part of his brain wanted to grab one of her hands and lace their fingers together, but he didn't dare. "I can give her back if you want."

She smiled. "I'll let you lug her around. I swear, the bigger she gets the harder it is. I need to add some muscle if I'm going to keep carrying her everywhere."

"You're perfect the way you are." He cringed at his words, but the way her grin widened before she dropped her gaze to the sidewalk told him she enjoyed the compliment. "How are you holding up? You've been through a lot the last couple days," he said, needing to change the subject.

She shrugged. "I'm okay. Not knowing where Bill might be, waiting for him to pounce when the moment strikes, is nerve wracking. But I'm not sure if it's worse than the months I've spent locked away with him. Knowing where he was didn't make life any easier. Didn't help keep him from hurting me."

He fisted his free hand at his side. Marie was such a strong, amazing woman. How anyone could hurt her was beyond him, but the fact it was a man who not only left bruises on her but used her love for her family to chain her to him caused every tendon in his body to tense—hoping for a moment to exact a certain kind of revenge no lawman should dream about.

"I'm sorry for everything you've been through, but soon it will all be behind you. You and Nora can live your lives without always looking over your shoulder."

"It seems impossible that could be our future, but I hope you're right."

A few moments of silence passed between them. They turned onto Main Street, along the river. The past few days of rain kept most people inside, and even the shops had taken in their usual sidewalk displays, meant to lure customers indoors. The colorful umbrellas, often open to shade diners and those simply enjoying a view of the river, were all folded. The sound of rushing water reached Owen's ears even yards away from the railing that ran the length of the riverwalk.

"What about you?" Marie asked. "You've had a tough time. First with Pappy being shot then Tommy. That must weigh on you."

He blew out a long breath, trying to remember the last time someone had cared enough to ask after him. "Honestly, I haven't let myself stop and think about it. Pappy is tough as nails and too stubborn to let some punk like Bill keep him down. And Tommy... Well, I shouldn't have let him go up in that treehouse alone. But I don't have the luxury of wallowing in my guilt. Not when I have a killer to find."

"Admitting your feelings and checking in with yourself aren't luxuries," she said, bumping her shoulder against his. "They're necessary to keep moving forward. To not stumble on things left unsaid, things left undone."

Stopping, he faced her and tilted his head to the side. "I've never thought about it like that. I've always been of the mind to shove things down as far as possible, pretending everything's fine and just moving forward. No matter what."

"One day, you're going to explode. Either that or turn into a hermit like your grandfather. A sweet old man who's a little paranoid and afraid to let people in."

He winced. "Pappy's a good man, but you're right. He's never talked about the death of my mother, at least not in a healthy way. He's always been caught up in finding who drove the car that hit her. He's never stopped and dealt with his grief, or acknowledged his family needed him to be there for support."

She rested a hand on his forearm and frowned. "I'm sorry. I didn't mean to criticize Lewis. I think he's a wonderful man. But I do feel sorry for him. I hate that he's hidden and alone. It didn't take long for me to understand he pushes away people he loves. Who knows. Maybe I'd do the same thing if I lost my daughter."

The crack in her voice squeezed his chest. "As long as I'm around, I'll make sure you'll never have to worry about that."

Her grin came back. "I believe you. I don't know why, or even how it's possible, but I've trusted you from the moment I saw you."

"I hear that a lot," he said. "It's the badge."

She laughed and playfully slapped at his chest.

The heat of her palm seeped through his shirt, and he rested his hand over her knuckles, trapping her against him.

All humor fled from her face. Her eyes flew wide, her pretty lips slightly parted.

He swallowed hard, debating against being a gentleman and capturing her mouth in his and finally finding out how she tasted. He took the tiniest step forward, only allowing a whisper of space between them.

"Waaa!"

Nora's cries broke the magic of the moment.

A shy smile slid up the corner of Marie's mouth, and she lifted the blanket covering Nora's head. "What's wrong, baby? You want to see the world?"

The cries stopped. Nora smiled.

Owen's heart melted as disappointment swept in faster than the water flowing down the river. He should have made a move. Should have let his guard down and opened up to Marie. But now the moment had vanished.

He made a silly face at Nora, and the little giggle was the sweetest sound he'd ever heard. "All right ladies. Let's get lunch. I'm starving."

MARIE LEANED against the vinyl booth at Lulu's Diner and let the waitress place the full plate in front of her. Her stomach may be empty, but the scent of her chicken club sandwich didn't do anything to increase her appetite.

Not when the only thing she craved sat across from her.

Not when she couldn't stop thinking about the sad man who tried so hard to help a nephew who was drowning in grief.

"Thank you," she said and formed a puddle of ketchup beside her fries.

Owen mumbled something that sounded like thanks as he shoved a burger in his mouth.

The waitress laughed. "Let me guess, you haven't taken time

to eat today? You need to take better care of yourself." The petite brunette batted her long lashes and patted his arm before turning and sashaying away, her hips swinging with the motion.

Marie chanced a peek at Owen, but his focus remained squarely on the food heaped high on his plate and not the flirting server.

Something loosened in her chest. She had no reason to be jealous of the pretty woman, but she couldn't help it. Owen's complete lack of awareness of the server's attention lifted her lips.

Owen dipped his chin toward her untouched plate. "I promise, Lulu's serves the best food in town."

Marie swiped a fry and twirled it in the red goo. "Everything smells great. I'm just not very hungry right now."

Owen raised his brows. "Are you feeling okay? We haven't eaten since breakfast, and it's way past lunch time. You really need to eat something."

Nibbling on the end of the fry, she let the salty goodness explode on her taste buds and hoped it would reawaken her appetite. She glanced at Nora in her carrier beside her, and her stomach turned. "I'm fine. I just can't get Steven Piper's sad eyes out of my head. I understand what he's going through. I admire that he tried so hard to help his nephew, especially while dealing with his own loss."

Owen set down his burger and reached for her hand. "I'm sorry. I didn't even think of the similarities between him and Eddy and you with your mom. Do you want to talk about it?"

Marie shrugged and dropped her burning eyes to the large hand covering hers on the table. She hated to admit how much comfort such a simple gesture brought her.

She wished they could go back outside in the sunshine. Back to the silly banter and the anticipation that zipped through her when Owen had looked at her with a different kind of hunger. But the struggles of the past days, weeks, and months refused to be ignored. "There's not much else to say. I've told you all of it."

"A wise woman once told me it's a good idea to check in on your emotions." He squeezed her hand, sliding his fingers between hers.

Marie glanced into his hazel eyes and the kindness shining back at her stole the air from her lungs. "I feel like I'm stuck in some kind of movie and just going along with the motions. Heck, I've felt like that for a long time." She sighed. "But talking with Steven Piper about Eddy was different—the emotions ran much deeper for me. I feel bad for Eddy. He's just a kid who got dealt a crap hand and didn't know how to handle it. That could have been me or even Renee."

Owen tipped the side of his mouth in a half-smile. "We're all thrown something hard at some point in our lives. It sounds like Eddy had people willing to help, but he didn't want it."

A vise gripped her heart. "You're right, and I meant what I said about people needing to want help in order for it to work. I wish I'd had someone to offer me support. There are plenty of rehab centers around for addicts, and child protective services when things get really bad, but I just needed support. A place to go and escape the craziness of my life or people to help navigate the messed-up path I've walked my entire life."

Safe Haven Women's Shelter was there for people who needed a place to land while they got back on their feet. Could a shelter like that offer even more to a community? A place for people to turn to when abuse and the need for a roof or food weren't the only problems?

"You're an amazing person, and strong. It's not fair that people are born into crappy situations and have to fight just to survive. Something like what you described should exist, a support system for family of addicts. It's a darn good idea, and one I'm surprised we don't offer in our community. Lord knows there's a strong need for it." Owen ran a hand through his hair and twisted his lips. "But we all have to make the tough choices sometimes to come through the hard times. Sounds like Eddy had the support he needed—he just didn't accept it."

Marie sighed and picked up another fry. "But we all make dumb choices when we're younger. Not all of us come in to contact with a scumbag like Bill who exposes our weaknesses and strikes when we're vulnerable."

"What about you? You've known Bill since you were kids. How did you manage to not get caught up in his drama?" Owen pulled back his hand and grabbed his glass of soda, taking a sip before setting the drink back on the table.

Marie lifted a shoulder and sighed. Her past with Bill was so darn complicated. "Like I said before, he wasn't so bad when we were kids. He was tough, had to be the way we grew up, but he didn't get into trouble until high school when his dad left. When I found out my mom helped hook him up with a dealer, I broke up with him. I couldn't handle one more user in my life. But he was always around, and I checked in on his mom a lot after she got sick. I think Bill always thought that meant I wanted to be with him still, but I just cared for her and wanted to make sure she was all right. Her death was a turning point. He cracked, and I stayed as far away from him as possible. Unfortunately, it wasn't far enough."

Owen's phone pinged, and he shot her an apologetic look. "I need to check this. Could be important." Shifting to gain access to his front pocket, he retrieved the phone and studied the screen.

Dread pooled in her stomach, and she dropped the uneaten food in her hand. "What is it?"

Owen's lips moved silently as he read whatever was on his phone. "My dad sent an email. He and Tommy went through Erica's work computer and passed along some files. Said it looks like something fishy is definitely happening at the school."

Marie sucked in a breath and closed her eyes. Leave it to Bill to prey on teenagers for profit, but it still didn't explain who he had connections with in Water's Edge. She opened her eyes and focused on Owen. "Did they find anything about Damon?"

"Doesn't say. I need to pull up these files on a bigger computer to get more in-depth information, and then I need to speak to Principal Teller. If something is going on at the school, she needs to know."

Marie glanced at the round clock on the wall. School was almost over for the day. How had the hours slipped by so quickly? "Another trip to the school?"

Owen shook his head. "No. I want to glance through some of this before we visit Ms. Teller. We'll swing by the sheriff's department then stop by her house. Sometimes people give more information when they're not expecting you."

A shiver raced down her back that had nothing to do with the vent blowing cold air on her. Maybe Ms. Teller knew more than she realized, or maybe she was an expert about keeping her secrets hidden.

17

A bright teal door with a brass knocker stood in stark contrast to the white colonial house with black shutters in the historic part of town. Owen had always loved walking along the red brick road as a child, following behind Katherine who pretended the path would take her to a grand wizard instead of across the street to the towpath.

He didn't have time to dwell on silly games and fantasies now as he stood outside of Ms. Teller's home, the rain returning. He only had time for facts and answers. Especially with Marie and Nora waiting in the car.

Swinging the knocker against the door, his nerves tingled, a sign he was close to figuring out this nightmare. But certain pieces were missing—pieces Erica Zyler took to her grave. The files he'd scanned were full of random notes and numbers that meant nothing.

She'd also noted the amount of drug related deaths in the area, an alarming number coming from teenagers over the last four weeks. But one thing was certain, Erica had focused her investigation on Water's Edge's High School and its faculty, something that made the burger in Owen's stomach turn to lead.

Owen stilled his muscles and listened for signs of activity inside the house. A garage door rattled open. He jumped from the front stoop and followed the sound to the attached garage. The garage door slid open, exposing unorganized clutter. That'd explain why the car sat in the driveway and not tucked inside where Ms. Teller would be protected from the constant rainfall.

A woman stepped out of the house, her back to him as she flipped on the light in the garage.

"Ms. Teller?" Owen asked.

The woman whirled around with a hand pressed to her chest. Patricia Teller stood with wide eyes, her brown hair pulled back in a stubby pony tail. "Oh, my goodness. You startled me. Is that you, Deputy Wells?"

He stayed on the edge of the driveway, not wanting to intrude on her personal space without an invitation. "Yes, sorry to scare you. I just received some more information on my case, and I wanted to run some things past you. I hope that's okay."

"Yes, please come in. I was just about to put together some pots." She tipped her head toward a long wooden bench on the far side of the space. Pots of multiple shapes and colors nestled on the floor, and gardening tools and flats of colorful flowers took up the space on the bench. "It's been too wet to do much in my garden outside. I thought it'd be nice to get my hands a little dirty inside instead."

He wandered inside and studied the bright petals. "The flowers are nice."

Ms. Teller smiled and pulled on a pair of dirty gardening gloves. "Thank you, but I'm sure you're not interested in my petunias. What brings you by?"

Owen bounced his gaze around the mess of scattered tubs and holiday decorations and tried not to cringe. "I obtained some information regarding overdoses in the area of high school-aged kids. Is this an issue you've been made aware of?"

Ms. Teller nodded, a deep frown on her face. "Yes, of course. We've been lucky. I'm not naïve. I'm sure some of the students dabble in those types of activities, but we haven't experienced any overdoses. Some of the principals from local schools have even reached out and wanted to know our secret."

He tilted his head and studied the concerned ripples across her forehead. "What did you tell them?"

She shrugged. "We have no secret. Just good kids from good homes."

"What about Eddy Jones?"

Ms. Teller sighed. "The exception to the rule, I suppose. Like I said, we tried to help him. He's been through a lot, especially at such a young age. I know that's not an excuse, but it's got to count for something."

Eddy's hardships might be hard to swallow, but Ms. Teller was right, it didn't excuse his horrible decisions. They'd already discussed Eddy. He needed a different tactic if he wanted to gain new information. "Did you hear Damon Silas was shot?"

Ms. Teller gasped and covered her mouth with her hand. She winced and dropped the dirty glove-covered hand to her side. "What happened?"

"I can't discuss the specifics, but the timing is suspicious. First Eddy is connected to assorted crimes, then the one teacher you claim was able to get through to him was gunned down. Would Eddy have an axe to grind against his teacher? Was their relationship ever inappropriate?"

Ms. Teller shook her head and picked up a small pot from the ground, placing it in front of her on the potting bench. "Never. Mr. Silas is a great teacher and a nice guy. He tried everything to help that boy."

"Have there been any complaints, from parents or students, regarding Mr. Silas?" Owen asked, taking a step closer.

Ms. Teller busied her hands with soil and flowers, taking her time in answering the question.

Silence wove through them and caused tension to pulse in Owen's head. "Even if it was a little complaint, something that seems petty or of little consequence, you need to tell me."

Ms. Teller drew in a deep breath. "Mr. Silas has taken more time off than usual the past month. I try to be lenient when staff needs personal time, and I figured he had a good reason for needing it. A couple different substitutes have taken over his class, and there have been a few complaints about missing equipment."

Owen's heart kick-started into high gear. "Why didn't you tell us this yesterday?"

Ms. Teller swallowed hard. "I didn't think it mattered. Students lose or break things all the time."

Owen swore under his breath and shook his head. Frustration rippled through him. "Thank you for your time."

He turned to leave, and something caught his eye in the corner of the room. A wooden crossbow sat tucked beside a black tarp. Pivoting to face Ms. Teller, he fought the muscles that threatened to display his emotions on his face. "Do you hunt?"

Ms. Teller laughed. "Absolutely not."

He nodded toward the corner. "Then why do you have a bow?"

Ms. Teller lifted herself on her toes to glance in the direction he indicated and shrugged. "When my ex took off, he left behind a lot of his stuff. He liked to hunt. Must have forgotten he had that in here."

Owen pressed his lips together. "All right. Let me know if you think of anything else that could be of use."

He rushed to his car as a clap of thunder boomed in the distance. A storm was coming, and he needed to be prepared.

Something told him Ms. Teller was in the eye of the impending hurricane.

SILENCE LOOMED over the house Marie had grown to love. Once they'd returned to Lewis', Katherine left and Marie settled Lewis and Nora in for the evening. The bond she shared with the ornery old man ran deeper with every passing hour. Leaving him would be hard when all this was over—almost as hard as leaving Owen.

Darkness blanketed the living room, the only light bursting from the laptop on Owen's thighs. Marie ran a hand over her tangled strands of hair and stepped into the room. She turned on the lamp on the end table and sent a soft glow around the space.

She loved the simple comforts of this warm home. The worn rug on the floor, framed pictures of kids cluttered on every available surface, and antique furniture in cheerful tones.

Luxuries of any kind didn't exist in the trailer she'd grown up in. Whatever money she made went to essentials—food, electricity, clothes. Whatever her mom earned fed her habit before her children. Crocheted blankets and pink depression-ware bowls filled with old candy were as far from her world as the moon and the stars.

Settling beside Owen, she tried not to stare open-mouthed at his sexily-tousled hair and the tight fabric stretched over his toned biceps. God, she hoped drool didn't linger at the corner of her mouth. "Find anything useful?"

The crooked grin he shot her was just full enough to enhance his dimples. "No. I can't find anything about who Patricia Teller dated. She has no marriages on record. Nothing else I've found stands out."

"Is there anything I can do to help?"

Owen leaned forward and grabbed a pink notebook from the coffee table. "How about you glance through the journal, while I navigate the budget from the school?" Owen handed her the book they'd found in Erica's apartment.

She ran the top of her finger along the smooth cover. Had Erica scribbled everything she thought could be important in this book, or just key information? Had she spent hours pouring over every word the same way she had over the past months in her own notebook?

Straightening, Marie faced Owen and allowed herself one little peek at his broad shoulders before meeting his eyes. "Where's my notebook?"

Owen glanced around then palmed his face, rubbing the inside corner of his eye with his finger. "In my car."

She bit into her bottom lip, disappointed. She'd wanted to flip through both books and see if anything matched or something sparked a memory. "We can glance through it tomorrow, there's more than enough to look into tonight. It's rainy and dark—there's no telling if someone is outside lurking around." Her shoulders gave an involuntary shudder.

"I'll grab it. Lock the door when I step out. It will only take a second." Placing the computer on the couch, Owen stood.

Marie clenched her jaw to keep her mouth from falling open. Gray sweatpants hung low on his hips. Her nipples morphed into hard buds and pressed against the thin material of her tank top.

Owen caught her eye and smirked. "You'll have to stand to lock the door while I'm outside. Make sure to let me in when I come back. It's pouring outside."

"Of course." She rose on Jell-O–like legs, crossing her arms over her chest, and followed Owen to the door.

Slipping sneakers on his feet, he hurried outside, and rain drizzled through the thick crack between the house and the wood before Marie closed and locked the door. She peered through the rectangular windows. Storm clouds and the canopy of trees shrouding Lewis' house blocked the moon, making Owen a mere shadow as he leapt off the porch and ran to his car.

Apprehension tickled her spine. Bill had hidden earlier in the light of day in these woods. He could be out there now. Waiting for another chance to strike. Despair settled on her chest like a weight. Maybe if she'd listened a little harder, paid a little closer attention, she'd remember something that could tell them where Bill was. There couldn't be that many options. He kept his circle small. It shouldn't be so difficult to find him.

Owen barreled back to the house and bounded up the stairs, skipping two steps on his way to the porch.

She flung open the door and stepped back to let him enter. She shut the door and secured the lock. Drips of water splashed from his finger-length hair and clung to his skin. The scent of an early summer storm swirled around him, and Marie took another step back before she did something stupid.

Reaching under his drenched shirt, he pulled out her notebook. "It's coming down hard. It got wet, but I took the worst of it. I need to change."

Marie grabbed the notebook, her fingers dipping into the soggy material of the cover. "Thanks."

He flashed her a grin. "I've got some old clothes in the spare room. I'll be out in a second."

Marie let her gaze stay locked on the wet shirt stuck against his broad back as he made his way down the hall and disappeared into the spare room. Man, she really needed to get a grip. Shaking her head, she crossed over the woven rug and made her way into the kitchen. She needed to find a dry dishrag or paper towels to dab the moisture off the pages before the water smeared the pen marks. She quietly rummaged through the cabinets until she found what she needed, blotted the cloth against the first moist pages, then returned to the couch.

Owen sauntered back into the room and settled in beside her. A stab of disappointment pierced her that his dry clothes didn't cling to his body.

Marie flipped open Erica's journal to the first page. Just as Owen mentioned earlier, random letters and numbers littered the lines. Some letters made up words, others didn't. No way she could make heads or tails of any of this mess. Not like it mattered if her instincts were correct, and the page contained passwords they didn't need any more since someone stole her computer.

Marie flipped to the next page. She used the tip of her finger to scan the lines of information, not wanting to lose track of what she'd already read. Names and places and random thoughts blurred together, but nothing triggered a memory.

This was a waste of time. She had no idea what she was looking for, so how would she ever be able to help? Owen probably had a whole system figured out and was trying to make her feel useful by giving her busy work.

On a sigh of frustration, she turned to the next page and the bottom dropped out of her world. Tears stung her eyes, and her hand shook as she lifted it from the page and pressed the back of her hand to her mouth. A tortured noise flew from her covered lips.

"Marie? Is everything all right?"

She shook her head, her gaze fixed on the page in front of her. "No. Erica has my mother's name written down."

Anger pushed Marie to her feet and she paced, her strides taking her across the room and back quickly. The pretty pictures and charming clutter that had grabbed her attention earlier faded to the background.

All she saw was red.

Ragged breaths tore through her body, and she bit into the

sides of her cheeks. She wanted to cry and scream and squeeze her hands around her mother's neck.

But she wouldn't do any of those things. At least not right now.

"I'm so stupid," she groaned. "I really thought she'd changed this time—that she was staying clean and getting her life on track."

"Calm down for a second. We don't know why Erica made note of your mom's name. It could mean anything."

She stopped and narrowed her eyes to study him. "Do you really believe that?"

Owen shrugged. "I have to keep an open mind. If I jump to conclusions, I might miss something. Besides, who would your mom know in Water's Edge to connect Bill with? Why bring him here?"

Marie threw her hands in the air. "Apparently, I don't know anything about the woman, so how should I know?"

A sob tore through her throat, but she choked it down and covered her mouth with her hand. "Oh my God. She set this whole thing up. She sacrificed me to Bill to get her grubby hands on money and more drugs. How could she?"

Owen stood and closed the distance between them, placing a heavy hand on each of her shoulders. He dipped his head, forcing her gaze to meet his. "I understand you and your mom have a complicated history, but don't go there yet."

"Do you really think there's another explanation?" She hated the hope in her voice, but believing her mom had thrown her to the worst wolf of all would break her.

"I honestly don't know." He squeezed her shoulders and lifted his lips at the corners. "But there's no reason to get upset before you know all the facts. It looks like Erica's done quite a bit of homework. She'd have known you lived with Bill, so maybe she checked your background."

His words made sense, and she clung to them like a lifeline.

The rage building inside her died down, taking the tension from her muscles. She melted against him, needing the hardness of his body for support.

This whole day had been too much. As much as she wanted to help, right now she wanted an escape, a distraction from the horrible shape her world had taken. If she didn't allow herself a minute to get a handle on her emotions, she would collapse into a puddle of tears.

Owen slid his arms around her neck, pulling her close to his body.

The same sense of peace and safety he'd given her earlier returned, and she wrapped her arms around him. The smell of the rain still clung to his skin. His heart raced under her ear. She let the rapid *thud, thud, thud* calm her nerves. With each steadying inhale through her nose, she breathed him in. She spread her hands wide across his back and tilted her head so her chin rested on his chest.

His Adam's apple bobbed. He stood absolutely still, as if afraid of what he might do if he moved, his muscles tight under her touch.

Marie bit her lip. He was so close. All she'd have to do was lift herself up on her toes and press her lips to his. Common sense battled with raw desire.

He dipped his chin and fire burned in his hazel eyes.

She swiped her tongue across her top lip, folded her hands at the base of his neck, and angled him down to meet her.

His lips brushed against hers, soft and sweet, and he molded her against him.

Her reaction was so strong, so instant, she wanted to run, but only hung on tighter as courage sparked inside her. She pressed her tongue into his mouth, licking inside his warmth. The minty taste of him exploded on her taste buds, and she pressed harder, sealing her mouth to his.

Owen moved his hands down her back and matched each

thrust of her tongue with more intensity, more urgency. He secured his palms at the base of her spine and dipped the tips of his fingers under the waistband of her shorts, skimming her sensitive skin.

Fire raged inside her, and she wiggled against him. The hard length of him pressed into her stomach. She wanted—needed—more.

Owen reared his head back, breaking their kiss, and hissed through his teeth. Leaving one hand lingering on her backside, he cupped his other hand around her neck. His rapid pants sounded through the quiet room, and his chest rose and fell with every breath. Leaning forward, he rested his forehead on hers. "Marie."

He said her name as if speaking a prayer, the whisper of his breath warm against her cheek.

"We can't do this here," Owen said through clenched teeth. "God, I want to more than you know, but you deserve better. You deserve a suite at the Ritz and me sweeping you off your feet, not trying to be quiet so we don't wake my grandpa."

Marie tried to pull away. Humiliation scorched her cheeks. This was why he hadn't kissed her earlier. She'd misread him, misread everything.

Owen slipped his hand into hers and refused to let her escape.

Closing her eyes, she tried to calm her sputtering heart and gain some control of her emotions. Acting so brazenly was completely out of character, and his rejection stung, even if his tender words helped soothe her injured pride.

Long fingers lifted her chin. "Hey. Look at me."

She opened her eyes and hoped her disappointment didn't shine through. A lump wedged in her throat.

Trailing his fingers from her chin to her jawline, he grazed her skin with his thumb. "I don't know how it's happened so quickly, but you mean a lot to me. I don't want to hurt you by rushing into something. Especially with so much going on. Not only has the past few days been one scare after another, but you just had the shock of seeing your mom's name written down by a murdered woman you never met. Let's take a second to catch our breath before we jump into something you might regret."

She nodded and sucked in a large breath. Instead of hiding in her room, she needed to pretend like his rebuff hadn't affected her. "You're right. Instead of running from my problems by kissing you, we should figure out what Erica knew about my mom."

His jaw tightened and his pupils dilated for a second before a small smile lit his face. "Then it's settled. We'll dive into what we were working on. That should take precedence anyway."

Freeing her hand from his, she hurried to the couch and sat, tucking her feet beneath her. She'd rather burn alive than be so exposed. She grabbed Erica's notebook and ignored the dip of the cushion beside her, the brush of Owen's shoulder against hers. She flipped a few more pages, searching for another mention of her mother's name, but found none.

A sliver of relief wedged itself inside her, but she tried to smash it. Her mother's name was written down for a reason, and she needed to know why.

Using the tip of her finger to underline the unfamiliar handwriting, a different name caught her eye. "Owen, Ms. Teller's first name is Patricia, right?"

"Yes." The word came out low and husky and sexy as hell.

She cleared her throat in an attempt to rid all the ridiculous lust from her system. "I wonder if she ever goes by Pat? Erica's mentioned that name a few times." She handed him the journal.

Owen's phone buzzed on the table in front of them, and he grabbed it and checked the screen. He pressed the phone to his ear and a high-pitched screech poured through the speaker. "Okay, hold on." He stretched his hand toward her and dipped together his brows. "It's your mom. She's upset, and I can't understand a word she's saying."

Marie bit back a groan. She should have never given his number to her family. She took the phone and emotionally steeled herself for whatever trouble her mother had found. "Mom? What's going?"

"She's gone. She should have been home hours ago." Wails dominated the speaker, jumbling her mom's words.

"Who, Mom? What are you talking about?" She tried to keep her voice calm. Feeding into her drama would only make her mom more upset.

"Renee! She didn't work today and should have been home after school. I've called the diner to see if she picked up a shift and no one's seen her. I've called, and she doesn't answer. She's missing."

Intense fear swept through Marie and she tightened her grip on the phone, locking her gaze with Owen. She sucked in a deep breath, surprised she was even able to breathe. "My sister. Bill has my sister."

18

Chills danced down Marie's arms, causing goosebumps to erupt over her exposed skin. Ragged breaths tore through her tight chest, and memory after memory of every horrible thing she'd suffered at Bill's hands flooded her mind.

Squeezing her eyes shut, she pressed a palm to her throat and fought the nausea churning in her stomach. Her mom's screeching voice assaulted her eardrum, but she couldn't make out her words, couldn't fight the fear suffocating her brain. She'd left town with Bill to protect her family, and now her sister was missing.

A gentle touch grazed her knee, and she locked her gaze on Owen.

Concern creased his forehead, but laser focus beamed from his narrowed eyes.

"Marie, take a breath. Calm down and tell me what happened." Kindness seeped into his no-nonsense tone and broke through the fog in her brain.

She blinked, filled her lungs with air, and cleared the cotton from her throat. She held up a finger, indicating she needed a moment. Before she could talk to Owen, she needed to calm her mom. "Mom, stop yelling. It's hard to understand you."

"I'm sorry. I'm just scared to death. This is so unlike her. I don't know what to do." Wanda's voice wobbled, as if she fought a losing battle against keeping tears at bay.

"Did you call any of her friends?" She clamped her free hand over Owen's, which still rested on her knee.

"No one has seen her."

Owen leaned forward. "Has she reported your sister missing?"

"Mom, did you call the police?"

"They said she hasn't been missing long enough to be declared a missing person, but they'll keep an eye out for her."

Marie cupped a hand over the speaker. "Mom called, but she's only been missing since this afternoon."

"Tell her you'll call her back. I want to get some information from you, and then I'll call the station. If they understand the situation we're dealing with, it will prompt them to take this more seriously."

Marie nodded, dropped her hand from the phone, and let his calm take-charge attitude keep her from jumping out of her skin. "I need to call you back, Mom. I'm with a sheriff's deputy right now from Water's Edge, and he wants to get more details about Renee and speak to the police back home himself. If you hear from Renee, call this number immediately."

"Okay. We have to find her. If something happens to her..." Weeping took over the line.

Marie's heart pounded in her ears and tears gathered at the corners of her eyes. "We'll find her. I promise." Her vow rang with false hope, but that was all she had to hold on to right now.

"I love you, honey." Exhaustion made Wanda's voice heavy, as if all the tears she'd cried weighed down her words.

Marie cleared her throat, but emotion clogged her windpipe. "I love you, too." She disconnected the call and fell forward, leaning against Owen's strong frame. He wrapped his arms around her, and she melted against him.

He rubbed his palm up and down her back. "Can you answer a few questions for me?"

She nodded against his shoulder, unable to speak and unwilling to pull away from the comfort of his arms.

"How long would it take Bill to get to your hometown?"

"Jackson Hill is only about two hours from here. Right outside Gatlinburg."

Owen's body tensed.

Marie slid from his embrace and narrowed her teary eyes, sniffing back any more moisture. She needed a level head to find her sister. She'd given herself a minute, but now she needed to pull herself together. "What is it?"

"Patricia Teller did her student teaching at a school in Gatlinburg."

"How long ago was that?" A heaviness settled into the pit of her stomach.

"Close to a decade ago. She worked at a school in the inner city. Did Bill spend time in Gatlinburg? Would he have dealt drugs there, or even had a supplier in the city?"

Marie pinched the bridge of her nose. "I don't know. I mean, it's possible. It takes no more than twenty minutes to get downtown."

"This definitely bumps Patricia Teller up on our suspect list. I want to talk to her again, but first I want to call and fill the police in on Bill and Renee." Owen hesitated and shifted his gaze to the side of her face, tucking a stray piece of hair behind her ear. "Is there anywhere else she might be? Friends your mom doesn't know about? A boyfriend she may have kept secret? Certain...activities you may not be aware of?"

Marie straightened and clenched her jaw. "What are you implying?"

Owen held his palms in the air. "Nothing, and I don't want to upset you. But we need to cover all the bases. If there's even a suspicion that she could be somewhere—even if it's hard to accept the possibility—now's the time to spill all."

His words were like a punch in the gut. Is that what he thought of her? If her mother was addicted to drugs, she and her sister would be, too? Did he assume Nora would end up with the same fate?

She ran her tongue over the top row of teeth. "My sister is a good kid. A hard worker and great student. She spends her time at school, work, and home. She's taken on way too much responsibility at a young age, and if she didn't go home right after school, there is a reason. If she isn't answering her phone and hasn't touched base with my mom, someone is stopping her from doing so."

Owen winced and reached for her hand, but she pulled away, no longer yearning for his touch. "I didn't mean to upset you. I had to ask, had to make sure I'm not leaving anything out when I make the call to the station."

She nodded, keeping her lips pressed together to stop the ugly words she wanted to yell. "I understand."

He dipped his chin toward his laptop. "Why don't you keep looking into Patricia? I focused my search more on the present and recent past. Maybe if we go back a little further, we can find the connection we've been looking for. Meanwhile, I'll also call my dad. I want to update him, and maybe he can figure out a way to get us a warrant for Patricia's house."

Marie stretched toward the laptop on the other side of Owen's lap, and he stopped her by wrapping his strong arms around her and tucking her against his side. He lifted her chin, and she couldn't stop the tickle of awareness his close lips brought.

"Don't be mad. Please. I want to find your sister, and to do that I have to ask the tough questions. If your sister is anything like you, she's a remarkable young woman, and I can't wait to meet her." He pressed a quick kiss to her lips then punched in some numbers on his phone.

A small bit of tension slipped from her shoulders.

Owen was a good guy. Her emotions were on high alert, and she'd overreacted to his question. He'd move mountains to help find Renee. She just hoped they found her before the worst happened.

OWEN PUSHED himself off the couch and paced across the worn rug that took up most of the living room floor. He needed distance from Marie to keep his brain working. The hurt in her eyes when he asked about her sister flashed in his mind, and he shook his head as he waited for his dad to answer the phone to get it out of his head.

He glanced over his shoulder. She sat straight with a rigid set to her shoulders he'd never witnessed. The clanking of keys floated from the computer as if she pounded her frustration on his keyboard. She might have understood why he asked what he had, but she definitely wasn't happy about it.

"Hey, Owen. What's going on?" His dad's words were thick, as if he spoke around a yawn.

Owen tore his gaze from Marie and continued his long strides. "There've been a few developments. Is Tommy with you?"

Mike snorted. "Yeah, and he's not happy about it. I wanted to keep an eye on him tonight, so I guilted him into staying at my place."

"Well put him to work. It'll take his mind off of being annoyed."

"What do you need?" All hints of exhaustion fled from Mike's voice.

Owen bit back a chuckle at his dad's new alertness. Mike Wells was all cop. "I need you two to dig up as much as you can about Patricia Teller."

"The high school principal?"

"Yes. Marie and I stopped by her place tonight and spotted a primitive bow in her garage. If we can tie her to the feather in the woods, we could have enough probable cause to search her house. She claims the bow belonged to her ex, who moved out, but I haven't found any information about men she's dated. Look into her past, go back to her college years and directly after graduation."

"Any particular reason?"

"She did her student teaching at an inner-city high school in Gatlinburg. Bill Flanders is from a suburb of Gatlinburg, Jackson Hill." His gut clenched, hating that he hadn't searched Patricia's work history sooner. "The connection we need could go back a decade."

Mike whistled. "Good work. No way all these overlaps are a coincidence."

"My thoughts exactly, but it's not enough for a warrant. I also want you to call Steven Piper and find out if he checked his work sites. He said he'd reach out to his supervisors to make sure no one's staying at any of his unused properties. My gut tells me the guy was a straight shooter, but I need that verified."

"The kid could break into a construction site without his uncle knowing."

"Absolutely, and if he's there, we need to find him immediately. Marie just found out her eighteen-year-old sister is missing, and she thinks Bill took her." The *click-clack* of keys stopped, and Owen pivoted to lock eyes with Marie.

Tears hovered over her lashes, and she pressed together her pretty pink lips.

Mike sucked in a breath. "She's sure he has her? There are no other possibilities?"

Owen believed Marie's gut, but he weighed his words, aware of her listening. He was trained to look at all options and not jump to the quickest conclusion. "I'm going to call her hometown police station next. The urgency of this case just increased tenfold."

"We're on it. I'll be in touch."

Owen turned his back to Marie and took a few steps in the opposite direction, keeping his voice low. "One more thing. When this is all over, I want to talk to you about starting something in town to help family members of addicts."

"You mean like AA for family?"

Owen shook his head, even though his dad couldn't see him. "Not really. That's a great program, everyone needs a safe space to share their experiences with people who can empathize. But more of a community outreach thing."

He needed to prove to Marie that he believed in her, even if her feelings didn't match his. She might have fallen into his arms and kissed him earlier to run from her problems, but he wanted to show her that she was more than just a distraction for him. For the first time since his mother's death, he wanted to open himself up to the possibility of a real relationship.

He wanted to open himself up to Marie.

"Okay. We'll talk later."

Owen disconnected, searched for the phone number he needed, then made his next call.

"Jackson Hill Police Station. How can I help you?" The words came from a gravelly, low voice and didn't hold a lot of friendliness.

Owen glanced at the clock on the ancient VCR Pappy insisted on keeping below the tube television. 9:45. "This is Sheriff's Deputy Wells from Water's Edge. I spoke with Detective Blough a few days ago about Bill Flanders. I need to be connected with whoever spoke with Wanda Robinson this evening about her missing daughter, Renee."

"One second please."

Owen faced Marie, who'd placed the laptop beside her and watched him with wide eyes and barely controlled emotions. "Are they connecting you?"

He nodded.

"Tell them to forget all the ridiculous stuff my mom's put them through. She's not the most credible person, so I understand why they'd brush off her concern. But this is different. I feel it in my bones." Her voice cracked, and she dropped her head in her hands. Her shoulders shook on silent sobs.

He ached to reach for her, kiss away her tears and comfort her, but the annoying elevator music stopped and someone clicked on the line. "Officer Pearlman. What can I do for you?"

"This is Deputy Wells. Are you the officer who spoke with Wanda Robinson?"

"Yes, sir. The girl's been missing since this afternoon, approximately seven hours. That's not enough time to declare her a missing person. Not to mention Renee Robinson is eighteen years old. It's not uncommon for kids that age to run around with friends without letting their parents know where they are."

Owen rubbed the back of his neck. This was what he'd been afraid of—that Renee had been missing for who knew how long and not a darn thing had been done to find her. "Are you aware of the situation we're dealing with in Water's Edge right now with one of your citizens?"

"I can't say that I am."

Owen bit back a sigh. "Bill Flanders is on the run and wanted for murdering a young woman a few nights ago. He's also suspected of dealing drugs in the area. We've been unable to locate him, and it isn't far-fetched to believe he'd return to his hometown. It's also suspicious that the sister of Marie Robinson, the woman who Bill Flanders has an abusive history with and who's been under my protection, goes missing."

"Crap."

"My thoughts exactly. I believe Renee Robinson is not just an irresponsible teenager who forgot to tell her mom where she was. Bill Flanders wants to use her to hurt Marie, and we need to find her now."

"I agree. I'll call Mrs. Robinson and get more details right away and send out an alert to all the officers in the area. With her history, I should have taken her more seriously."

His statement piqued Owen's interest. He'd assumed Wanda's call to the station would have eyes rolling at the dramatic worries of a drug-addicted woman who was known to cause problems, not garner more attention.

"Why should you have taken her more seriously? I know her history of drug use. Has she had issues with dealers harming her or her children to get money or send a message?" He'd seen it before—addicts who took more than they could afford to pay then suffered the consequences later.

If Marie's suspicions of why Erica Zyler had researched her mother were true, her inability to pay her debts could be what led both her daughters to danger. Marie would be crushed if her mom's addiction put Renee in harm's way, and she wasn't there to keep her sister safe.

A beat of silence pulsed on the line. "No...there are other reasons. Reasons I can't go into right now."

Owen opened his mouth to ask more questions but knew it'd be a waste of time. "Make your call to Wanda, and I'll be in touch."

Marie shot to her feet and knotted her hands at her waist. "I want to go home. I need to be with my mom, and maybe there's something I can do to help."

Hesitation slowed his response. He needed to be close to town to work the case, but if Bill went back to his hometown, it couldn't hurt to pay a visit to Jackson Hill. The drive wasn't too long, and if he could help find Renee it'd be worth the time spent away from the case.

"I'll drive you. Gather your stuff and I'll get Nora ready. We'll leave as soon as we can."

Appreciation shone through her panic, and she threw her arms around his neck. "Thank you." Pulling back, she pressed her lips to his than hurried off to the guest room.

His phone rang in his hand. A beat of hope pulsed through him. Maybe Renee had already been found. "Wells, here."

"Deputy Wells, we found Edward Jones."

Adrenaline pumped through his veins. If they had Eddy, they could find Bill, and hopefully, Renee. "Good, bring Eddy to the station for questioning."

"We can't do that, sir. Edward Jones is dead."

19

Owen pushed the gas pedal to the floor and flew down the gravel lane. Loose pebbles pelted the side of his car, and rain crashed down on his windshield. The wipers sped back and forth, unable to keep the hoard of rain from blocking his view. Breaking at the end of the driveway, he swiveled his neck to check for traffic then peeled onto the dark, wet road.

He'd already placed a call to his dad and Tommy, who would meet him at the address he'd provided, and Katherine was on her way to the house in case Pappy woke. Marie and Nora were with him, ready to head back to Jackson Hill as soon as he finished with the death scene.

"I can't believe he's dead," Marie said from the passenger seat, her voice barely audible against the onslaught of rain pounding against the roof. "He was so young."

A twinge of sadness twisted his stomach, but he ignored it. He couldn't let his sympathies for a young man caught up in a dangerous game cloud his judgement. "I feel bad for his mother. First her husband, and now this."

"What does this mean for Renee?" She groaned. "Does

asking that make me an awful person? A boy is dead, and I'm worried about how that affects my sister."

Owen tightened his grip on the wheel, needing to keep control of the speeding car on the water-covered road. "It makes you human, and I don't know what it means for Renee."

"Do you think Bill killed him?"

Owen shrugged. "Maybe. Or it's whoever else is involved in this mess. We've asked a lot of questions the last couple days, pushed a lot of people. If we got too close to the truth, someone besides Bill might have snapped—felt pressured to make a move to get us off their trail."

"Patricia," Marie said on an inhale of breath. "You asked her about the bow. It had to tip her off."

Owen nodded and turned toward town.

The house Eddy was found at wasn't far from Patricia's home. He still didn't know what had alerted the police to anything suspicious in the residence, but his nerves trembled to find the answers. Ignoring the speed limit signs posted at the city limits, he raced forward.

His tires caught on a large puddle of water swallowing the street, and his vehicle skid to the side. He took his foot off the gas and let the car slow, the tires regaining their grip on the asphalt.

The sound of heavy panting caught his attention, and he glanced at Marie. She pressed one hand against her heart while the other held a death grip on the door handle. Her eyes were squeezed shut, and her pale skin shone bright in the dark car. "Are you all right?"

She nodded, still not opening her eyes.

If he wasn't on his way to a murder scene, he'd stop the car and figure out what was wrong, but he didn't have the time right now. "Marie, talk to me. What's going on?" He returned his focus on the road and continued toward the resting place of Eddy Jones.

"I'm sorry. It's stupid." The breathy quality of her voice echoed with panic.

"Whatever it is, you can tell me." He shot her what he hoped was a reassuring look, but all the turmoil boiling in his gut made it impossible to smile.

She sighed. "I was in a car accident when I was younger. My mom drove into a lake. I still get nervous around water and am jumpy in cars. It's one of those traumas that stays with you, I guess."

Owen slowed, not wanting to heap any more stress on Marie's shoulders. "Is that why you asked about the flooding yesterday?"

"Yes, but my phobias are the least of our worries right now."

He wanted to argue, to let her know any fear she had was well-founded and something he'd help her get through, but she was right. He turned onto a side street, and the flashing blue and red lights put an exclamation point on that fact. Right now, he needed to concentrate on finding out who killed Eddy and why. He maneuvered the car into the driveway behind the squad car with the flashing lights and shifted into park. He faced her. "I need you and Nora to stay in the car. I'll be as quick as possible, and then we can concentrate on what we need to do to find Renee."

She swallowed hard and nodded. "Okay."

He raised his brows, expecting more of a fight. "Okay?"

"I get it. You need to go in there and do your job, and honestly, I don't want to expose Nora to whatever's in that house, no matter her age. I'll call my mom and see if she's heard anything more about my sister."

He reached behind the seat for the bag he'd brought containing what he'd need to examine the scene. "Keep your phone out in case you need to call me. I won't be long."

She nodded and the whites of her eyes lit through the darkness.

Pushing open the door, he hunched his shoulders and ran through the rain to the front of the house. An officer stood guard and opened the door after recognizing Owen. He stepped inside and wiped the lingering drops of moisture from his face.

He strode to the far corner of the barren room where a white sheet draped over a corpse laid in the corner, and two officers stood hunched over notebooks. The metallic scent of blood hung heavy in the air. "What do we have? Is the coroner on his way?"

The two officers glanced up from their notes with solemn eyes and grim sets to their mouths.

The younger cop, a fresh-faced man who made Tommy look old, took a step forward.

Owen racked his brain for the man's name but couldn't pull it forward.

"I was called to the scene. The caller claimed to be a neighbor who made a noise complaint. Said he heard screaming and what sounded like an abusive situation. When I got here, the house was quiet. I knocked and announced myself, then proceeded into the residence. The body was laying on the floor."

Sickness settled in Owen's stomach. "Any clue as to cause of death?"

The young man ran his tongue over his lips. "The deep slice across the victim's neck indicates a knife wound, my guess is inflicted by someone the victim knew. The medical examiner will know more, but there don't appear to be any defensive wounds."

"Strange if there was fighting going on." The complaint made didn't add up with what was found on the scene.

Owen hoped the officer's assessment was correct. Eddy might have made bad decisions that hurt a lot of people, but Owen wished the kid hadn't had to die—and he definitely hoped Eddy hadn't experienced a violent death. The only small grace would be if Eddy was asleep when it happened, none the wiser of what was to come.

He drew in a shuddering breath. "Did you clear the rest of the house?"

"Yes, sir. No sign of forced entry, and no other person on the premise."

Owen nodded. "Okay. I want you to go over every detail of what happened once you arrived on scene, and I'd like to see your notes. Then I'll take a look around." He dipped his chin toward the second officer standing quietly in the background. "I want you to talk to the neighbors. Find out who made the call and ask if anyone saw anything that happened here tonight. A car parked in the driveway, people coming and going from the house. Anything unusual."

Owen glanced down at the outline of Eddy Jones' body. He might not have found the kid in time to save him from himself, but maybe he could still get some answers.

MARIE GRIPPED the phone in her shaking hand. Rain splashed down on the car, making it hard to see the house Owen disappeared into. Saliva pooled in her mouth as her nerves danced around her body like a sugared-up child.

She was being silly. Owen was twenty-feet away, even if she couldn't see him.

A part of her wanted to march into the house, police protocol and grisly crime scene be damned. But the other part was afraid of what she'd find once inside. Enough gruesome images clamored in her brain—Pappy laying on the floor with a gunshot wound, Tommy passed out in the tree house, the blood-soaked carpet in the house she'd lived in for the past month—she didn't want to add another horrible memory to the bunch.

Didn't want Nora to absorb any of that negative energy.

Instead, she'd sit in the comfortable car and call her mother.

Punching in her mom's number, she shifted in the seat and kept her gaze locked on the door. An officer stood guard, adding to the little sense of security she had. She checked on Nora, sound asleep and oblivious to the danger around them.

The phone rang twice before her mom answered. "Hello? Marie, is that you?"

For the first time in as long as she could remember, relief flooded over her at the sound of her mother's voice. "Yes, it's me. Did you talk to the police again? Have you heard from Renee?"

"Still nothing, but I did speak to the officer at the station again. He asked me some more questions, and I gave him as many details as I could remember." Her mom spoke quickly—too quickly.

Marie constricted her grip and prayed her mom's fast-paced speech was due to nerves and not something she'd shot into her veins to take away her worry and fear. "Is he looking for her?"

"Yes. Thank the deputy you're with for stepping in. Hopefully, now that they believe me, they'll find her."

"I hope so," Marie said. She hadn't told her mom about her suspicions about Bill. If she was right—which she *knew* she was —her mom couldn't do anything to help. Being completely honest could possibly push her over the edge of her shaky sobriety...if she hadn't already jumped over that cliff.

"What happens now? Are you coming home? Maybe you can help find your sister?"

Tension squeezed her chest. "Hopefully, I'll be heading home soon."

"Good," Wanda said. "Then you and that grandbaby of mine can stay with me and things can go back to normal."

Normal—was that even a possibility after what she'd been through? She'd return to her dead-end job and keep her mom clean while caring for Nora, but she wasn't the same person she'd been when she'd left. She was stronger, wanted more from life.

She wanted Owen.

Her stomach muscles clenched. She had nothing to offer a man like him, not to mention nothing keeping her in Water's Edge. Staying here wasn't an option, unless she wanted to look like a clingy girl holding on to a dream that would never come true. Which as the last type of example she wanted to set for her daughter.

"I don't understand why you aren't already on your way home." The hard edge of her mom's voice caught her off guard.

Anger surged inside her. This entire situation was her mom's fault. "You wouldn't understand, would you? You've never managed to look past your own needs to see anything else clearly." Hysteria made the pitch of her voice so high it would cause dogs to bark.

"What are you talking about?" Her mom's confusion just pushed her further toward the breaking point.

She couldn't hold back any longer. Her mother's shaky sobriety be damned. "Everything is your fault. You're the reason I'm in this mess to begin with. You're the reason Renee is gone. If you could have just stayed clean and kept away from those stupid drugs, none of this would have happened. But you couldn't do that, could you? You couldn't put your family and your own well-being above the fix."

"Marie, honey, you don't understand. If you'd just let me explain."

Marie shook her head, unwilling to listen to the same lame excuses she'd heard her entire life.

A flash of movement caught her attention, and she shifted her focus back to the house.

The door opened and an officer stepped outside. He hurried down the sidewalk and crossed the lawn, the man who'd stood guard outside the door jogging into step beside him, to the neighboring house hidden behind a row of trees.

She leaned toward the driver's seat to gain a better view of the men but couldn't see anything though the heavy rain and barrier of tall branches and leaves. "I don't have time for this. I've got to go." She disconnected the call and tossed the phone on the seat beside her.

Tap, tap, tap.

Marie whipped around and her heart caught in her throat.

Bill stood at the rear of the car with her sister at his side, a gun pressed against her head. An idling car sat on the street behind him.

Lifting a finger to his lips, he crouched low and pushed her sister in front of him.

She kept her gaze locked on his, panic stealing her thoughts.

Bill stopped beside the passenger side and tried to yank open the door. A crooked grin dominated his mouth and rain streaked down his face. He pressed the gun against Renee's side. "Open it. Now." He mouthed the words.

Marie swallowed hard and did what he said.

He pulled the door open. "Don't even think about doing something stupid."

Marie curled her toes to keep from kicking her foot forward and slamming it into his shin. Bill would get a shot off before she could do any damage, and she couldn't risk Renee's or Nora's lives. She focused on Renee's sweet face. A purple ring circled her right eye. Hatred burned her chest, and her mouth went dry. She bit the inside of her cheeks to keep from crying. "Are you okay?"

Renee nodded, and Bill gripped her hair and yanked her head backward. "This isn't a reunion, it's an exchange. Get out of the car and come with me now, and I'll leave your sister here. If you refuse or try to run, I'll shoot her."

"Don't! He'll kill you!" Sobs ripped through Renee's voice. Tears mixed with the constant rainfall and coursed down her face.

Inching her fingers toward the phone, she shifted her gaze back to Bill. If she focused too much on Renee and the pain contorting her delicate features, she'd never find the strength to do what had to be done.

She'd never find the strength to leave Nora behind.

"I'll do whatever you want. Just don't hurt my sister."

Bill transformed his grin into a hard line. "Do you think I can't see you trying to grab the phone? Put your hands in front of you and get out of the car. Hurry up."

Desperation clawed at her throat, but when given a choice between her life or Renee's, Renee won hands down. And the faster she got out of the car, the better the chance Bill wouldn't ask about their daughter. Wouldn't notice the car seat in the back and demand she bring Nora with them.

Cold rain slanted into the interior of the car, drenching her clothes, but Marie was too numb to care. She stood on trembling legs and hugged Renee tight. She pressed her lips to her ear. "Nora's in the back. Please take care of her. I love you so much."

Renee clung to her, her slim body trembling.

"Enough. Get her in the car and let's go. If you try to scream or alert anyone to you being here, I'll kill Marie."

Marie's heart split in two. She broke away, pushed Renee down to the passenger seat, and slammed the door shut.

Renee shook her head, her tangled hair swirling around her face.

Bill pushed the hard barrel of the gun into her side. "Hustle to the car and don't be dumb, or I'll shoot you then go back for your stupid sister."

Marie held her chin in the air and did exactly what Bill told her. He'd won. He had her in his clutches and there was no way she'd fight him, not when the two people she loved most in this world were at risk.

She'd go with him, and when they were far enough away, she'd find a way to escape him once more.

20

T he scent of blood turned Owen's stomach. He wasn't used to the rich, irony scent and prayed he never would be. He stepped into the kitchen, waving the young officer to follow. Stale food and overflowing garbage added to the stench that clung to the dirty walls. "Looks like someone's at least made use of the kitchen. How's the rest of the house? Signs of people living here?"

The young officer grimaced as he scanned the small kitchen, just as bare as the living room except for the trash. "There's one bedroom with some clothes on the floor, and towels bunched up in the bathroom make me suspect someone's used the shower. I didn't get a chance to do more than glance around as I cleared the house before you showed up."

Owen extended his hand. "Can I see the notes you took?"

The officer handed over the small book.

Owen flicked his glance to meet the officer's cool blue eyes for an instant, then studied the messy handwriting on the pages. "Also, what's your name? I don't think we've worked together before."

"Officer Steele, sir."

Nodding, he continued to read the notes. The notes were meticulous, even if they didn't tell him anything more than the young man already had. He handed back the book and pulled a pair of gloves from his bag, yanking them over his hands. "Ever worked a death scene before?"

Officer Steele swallowed hard, keeping his gaze locked on Owen. "No, sir."

"Have you touched anything?" Owen arched his brows, dipping his chin toward Steele's uncovered hands clasped in front of him.

"No, sir. I have gloves in my pocket if you'd like me to help sweep the scene."

"Put 'em on. I have the deputies I'm working the case with on their way. Once they arrive, I'll need you to head outside and tape off the area." There was no telling if the killer would be back. He didn't want to be in the house alone if that happened, and having two people look through the house for evidence would get it done faster. Then he could get back to Marie.

Steele shoved his notes in his back pocket then donned a pair of gloves.

Owen could be a dick and make the younger officer scour through the disgusting kitchen for evidence. He glanced around and tightened his jaw to stop from sighing. He'd take the kitchen. If the rest of the house was as empty as the living room, chances of finding anything useful were slim—making the grime-covered kitchen the most likely place to find a clue. Better if he took it on himself. "Head back to the bedroom. It's a small house with not much stuff. Shouldn't take too long. Keep your eyes and ears open."

A glimmer of relief crossed over Steele's face before he headed out of the kitchen, his heavy footsteps bouncing off the worn hardwood floors.

Owen surveyed the kitchen and grimaced. A black garbage can sat in the corner, the kind that fits under the sink and barely had space enough to hold a day's-worth of trash. He crossed the room, the bottoms of his shoe sticking to some unknown substance on the floor. He checked his gag reflex and peered into the trash bin. Crumbled take-out bags and wadded paper towels spilled from the top and scattered on the linoleum floor.

A few scraps of loose paper caught his attention, and he dipped his hand inside to grab them. He unwrinkled the first. A receipt for a local fast-food restaurant. Time stamped the day before. He'd make a call to the restaurant as soon as possible and get access to their security feed. He retrieved an evidence bag from his duffle and secured the receipt.

He glanced at the other piece of paper. Garbled writing and smeared pen stared up at him. Nothing.

BEEP...BEEP!

The loud blast of a horn raised the hairs on his neck. He ran from the kitchen into the next room and shot toward the front door.

Officer Steele barreled down the hallway, his gun trained in his grip. "What's going on?" His pinched-together face displayed his concern, but he kept his voice calm.

"It's a car horn." Adrenaline zipped through him. The other two officers who'd been on scene when he'd arrived were canvassing the area, and as far as he knew, the coroner hadn't shown up yet for the body. The only person who'd blare a car horn was Marie, and she'd only do so if something was wrong.

"Keep your gun ready," he said over his shoulder as he gripped the knob and yanked open the solid wood door. "I don't know what's going on, but it can't be anything good. Be on your toes and stay close behind me."

He pushed open the white, rusted screen door, and rain splattered his face. He scanned the area, searching for anything alarming that would set off Marie. Red taillights flashed at the end of the road. The two officers he'd sent to the neighbors dashed through the yard.

BEEEEEPPP!!!

Launching off the square cement stoop, Owen sprinted toward his car. Something wasn't right. No one stood by the vehicle, but was someone inside? Had something spooked Marie that he couldn't see? His heart hammered in his chest and water splashed up from the unruly grass as he ran through the yard. He reached the car, gripped the handle, and locked eyes with a young woman he didn't know.

Shock paralyzed his limbs. He narrowed his gaze on the wide-eyed girl who seemed familiar, but he couldn't place her. He flicked his gaze beside her—no Marie. What the hell was going on?

Yanking open the door, the weeping girl recoiled.

The mark on her cheek screamed to his gut, and the mossy green of her eyes stole the air from his lungs.

"My sister...you have to save my sister." The words shook from her quivering chin.

"Renee?"

She nodded, and thick tears streamed down her cheeks.

"Where is she?" The woman he was falling in love with was likely in the hands of a murderer, and it was all his fault.

"Bill took her. He had a gun and told her if she didn't leave with him, he'd kill me. I told her no...told her to stay. She told me to take care of Nora." Renee pressed her hands over her mouth, and her voice broke, shoulders shaking.

Owen whipped back toward the road. The taillights had disappeared, the street empty. Marie was gone.

MARIE WHIRLED AROUND, the swift movement causing the water dripping from the ends of her hair to splash on her face. The sound of a blasting car horn caused hope to bloom in her chest. Pride mingled with the sliver of hope. Renee would get help one way or the other, but it might come too late.

She faced forward, glancing at Bill from the corner of her eye. The gun sat on his lap, and every muscle in her body screamed to grab the weapon. But she had to be smart. Her mind raced faster than the tires speeding across town.

Owen might be aware Bill had her, but the head start Bill secured might mean he wouldn't get to her before Bill did something stupid. She needed to get away from him, but hurtling through the mostly deserted streets in a car didn't give her many options. Maybe if he slowed down, she could throw herself from the vehicle and pray she survived the fall.

Keeping the side of her gaze on Bill, she slid her hand up the door and hooked her fingers around the handle. If the moment presented itself, she'd be ready.

Muttered curses flew from Bill's mouth. "You better hope your sister didn't just sign your death certificate. I told her not to be stupid, but I should have known better. She's as stubborn as you. I had to knock her around a bit to get her to listen." He reached over and squeezed her knee. "Reminded me of some good times."

Bile curdled in her stomach. She wanted to push his clammy hand off her skin, but she couldn't risk angering him more. What had happened to make him such a monster? Had it always been there, and she'd missed the signs? It didn't matter. She needed to focus on how to escape.

A flash of lightning lit the sky, highlighting the torrential downpour and showcasing the water pooling on the road. A different kind of fear shot through her. A fear rooted in a deep-seated memory. "Can you slow down? It's not safe driving so fast with so much water on the road."

Bill snorted. "Seriously? That's what you're worried about?"

She had so much to be concerned about it was hard to take her pick.

Not like it mattered, Bill had a one-track mind. He'd obviously do whatever he wanted without a thought to her concerns. "I'm worried about a lot of things. What about you? The police know what you did. They won't stop until they find you." She kept her voice calm and hoped the rain beating against the car drowned out the sound of her pounding heart. Bill fed off of fear. She couldn't let him see the shaking of her hands or hear the terror in her words.

"The police are idiots. No way they'll figure out where we're going. And once things die down a bit, we'll come back for Nora."

She chewed her bottom lip—there was no safe way to get out of this situation. No way she'd blindly follow along with whatever plan he had up his sleeve, and definitely no way she'd ever let him get his hands on Nora. "Will Patricia Teller meet us?"

Bill glanced her way with wide eyes and a clenched jaw. The car lurched to the side, and he flew his gaze back to the road, tore his hand from her knee, and righted the wheel. "What do you know about Pat?"

Marie's heart slammed up her throat, and she closed her eyes, taking deep breaths before she opened them again with steeled nerves. "I know she's in on whatever you and Eddy were doing. I know she's the reason you're here."

Bill curled his hands harder around the wheel and made the car go even faster. "She's an idiot. I never should have listened to her—should've stayed in Jackson Hill. Now I'm knee-deep in the mess she started."

Curiosity egged on Marie. Owen's comment came back to her. Patricia lived in their area a long time ago. "Why now? Why wait all these years before reaching out to you with her hairbrained idea?"

"My old man walked away from her like he walks away from everyone. Wanted something bigger than what they were doing in Gatlinburg. Pat could get most of the supplies from the school but didn't know how to mix them and couldn't risk selling. She thought she'd get the last laugh on my dear old dad, bring in his son, and increase sales at the same time."

Understanding dawned on her. No wonder Owen couldn't find information about Patricia's ex. If she was involved with a criminal, she'd make sure there was no trace of their relationship. "And you couldn't resist the opportunity to do something better than your dad. But why make me come with you? Why hold my mom's crimes over my head and force Nora and me to stay?"

"We're meant to be together. The way you've always taken care of my mom, of your family. I've loved you my whole life, and now we have a little girl to take care of." The tenderness in his voice took her by surprise.

Anger ripped through her. "You love me, but you made me leave my family then abused me and ignored your child. How do you even dare call that love? That's called kidnapping."

Bill swung his gaze to her and snarled. "I needed to show you I was the one in control, not you. I was the one with the power. If you'd just let me love you, shown me you wanted to be with me, I wouldn't have had to be so forceful. I took you away from a crappy life and wanted to give you a better one. You're too stupid to realize that."

Pure rage shook her limbs. She would not be his victim any longer, would not let him make her doubt who she was and what she was capable of. "You are an abuser," she said through clenched teeth. "None of what you did to me was my fault."

The pounding rain intensified, smothering the windshield. Terror clutched Marie's heart. She glanced out the window. A flash of water swept over the road. She squinted, trying to make out their location. A flash of yellow whizzed by. Was that the library? "Oh my God, the bridge is ahead. You need to slow down." Screw being calm, she yelled the words over the din echoing through the car.

"You need to shut your mouth."

The rain slowed enough for Marie to see clearly through the windshield.

"See," Bill said. "It's slowing down. Everything's fine."

The bridge came into view, rushing water churning below and crashing over the narrow lanes. Small rapids gurgled on the river, pushing faster and faster. The river was high—too high. Water flooded the road.

"You can't go over the bridge. It's not safe." Panic rose her voice an octave. She searched the car for something, anything, to help. She glanced at Bill and grabbed his forearm. "Please. Stop the car."

Bill pushed his foot to the floor and the car lunged forward. He shook off her hand from his arm. "Don't be dramatic."

She clutched the side of the door. She pressed her foot against the floor, as if she could make the car stop with an imaginary brake. The car barreled toward the bridge, Bill refusing to slow down. The tires slid along a patch of water and the back of the car fishtailed.

Marie gasped. "Take your foot off the gas. You have to slow down!"

"Sonofabitch." Bill yanked the wheel to the side, causing the car to spin toward the side of the road facing the edge of the river.

Marie tensed all the muscles of her body. "We're off the road. Stop the car. Now!"

"Shut up." Bill yelled over the beating rain and the spinning wheels. The tires gained traction on the muddy grass on the edge of the road and shot forward.

A scream ripped from her throat as they bounced on the uneven terrain and the car smashed into the frigid water.

21

Maire shot her arms in front of her, bracing herself against the impact. Her seatbelt pushed against her stomach. Water seeped into the car, soaking Marie's feet and raising to her ankles.

She squeezed the door handle and pushed her body against the hard metal door.

It didn't budge.

Tears blurred her vision as the water leaked through the frame. Chills raced up and down her goose-pimpled flesh, and her heart threatened to beat out of her chest. She smashed her finger against the button to lower the window, but it didn't move.

"Bill! What are we going to do?" She glanced at Bill, and ice filled her veins.

Bill slumped over the steering wheel, blood trickling from a wound on his temple. Wide, lifeless eyes stared back at her, and she swallowed the bile sliding up her throat.

Her hand trembled as she clicked the release of the seatbelt she'd thankfully secured. If Bill had thought to do the same, his outcome would have been much different. Sadness she didn't want to feel weighed down her heart. Bill had wasted his life on drugs and bad decisions. He could have done so much more.

Adrenaline ripped through her.

She wouldn't die like this—not when she had a beautiful baby who needed her. Not when she'd finally found a man who made her feel worthy of love.

Fisting her hands, she beat them against the window. Pain shot up her arms. Sobs shook her shoulders and the icy water rose—skimming her legs and collecting onto her lap.

She couldn't go through this again, couldn't feel the cold water sweep over her and steal her breath. No one should have to live through such a nightmare twice. Filling her lungs with air, she tried to calm her racing heart and figure out how to get out of the death trap before the car became completely filled. She rifled through the glove box, searching for something to break the glass.

Nothing.

The rain stopped and the moon peeked through the black clouds overhead, the bright light filtering through the windshield bounced off something shiny on Bill's lap.

The gun!

She grabbed the smooth metal, pointed the barrel at the window and pulled the trigger. Her ears rang as the bullet crashed through the glass, and water gushed through the hole, making the glass splinter until it shattered.

Water poured in with the force of a flash flood, filling the car with alarming speed. Marie lunged for the window. She gripped the edge of the car and hefted herself through the opening, but wave after wave pounded against her, pushing her back inside. The dirty river swallowed the inside of the car, consuming her.

She sputtered against the invasion against her face and drew in one last, deep breath before becoming completely submerged in the inky swirl of dirt and debris and water.

Her lungs burned and fatigue weighed down her limbs, but now that the car was filled and the pressure even, she had her chance at escape. She pushed her feet against the edge of the driver's side headrest and swam through the narrow window. The brown water impeded her vision, but she pressed her feet together and pumped them back and forth, raising toward the surface. She broke through the water and gulped in as much fresh air as her lungs would hold.

She bobbed in the river, continuing to kick her feet to keep her head above the rushing water. The current carried her downstream, and she swiveled her head back and forth to try to find the closest riverbank. The moon cast a dim light around her, but she couldn't lift herself high enough to gain a sightline on the shore. Running on instincts and adrenaline, she picked a path and swam, pushing herself past exhaustion in a fight to stay alive.

THUNDER BOOMED, and the storm intensified. Fear stole Owen's breath, but he couldn't give in to it—couldn't let it muddle his brain and cloud his judgement.

Renee stared up at him with wide eyes, her quivering mouth pressed in a straight line.

He glanced behind him. Officer Steele scanned the area with his gun poised for use. "Lower your weapon. I need you to look after this girl and the baby in the backseat."

Officer Steele dropped his arms and screwed his lips to the side. "Where do you want me to take them, sir? Inside the house?"

"No." Owen gestured toward the police car parked in front of his rental. "Is that your cruiser?"

Steele nodded.

"Sit in there. I don't want her to see what's in the house. Call the Jackson Hill police station and let them know we found Renee Robinson." Owen crouched down and focused on Renee. "Renee, I'm Owen, and I'm a friend of your sister's. I want to make sure you're all right, but I don't have time to waste. I need to go after Marie. Do you know what way Bill went? What kind of car he drove?"

"He's in a small blue car, but I don't know what kind. He mentioned heading back home." She set her jaw and kept her gaze locked on his.

"Okay. Take Nora and go with Officer Steele and wait in his car until I can get back. Tell him everything that happened. You can trust him, I promise."

He waited for Renee and Nora to get safely inside Officer Steele's vehicle then jumped into his own car. The engine still purred from when he'd left Marie earlier. Throwing the car in reverse, he shot toward the end of the driveway.

He scooped his phone from the passenger seat and called dispatch. "This is Deputy Wells. I need all available officers on the lookout for a blue sedan. Murder suspect—Bill Flanders—has kidnapped a young woman. He's considered extremely dangerous."

"Yes. sir."

Owen didn't respond, just disconnected, peeled out of the driveway, and took off toward the end of the road where red taillights had blazed moments before. Bill couldn't have gained much ground, not with the rain thundering down and water flooding the roads.

Water splashed up from the street, and he slowed his pace. He wouldn't do Marie any good if he got his car stuck in high water. He scanned the streets. Streetlamps shone down on empty sidewalks and deserted roads. Not many people were crazy enough to be out on a night like tonight.

A beam of light bounced to his left. On instinct, he turned

toward the headlights. He inched forward as fast as he dared. The car in front of him drove recklessly toward the bridge.

It had to be Bill.

Owen clenched the muscles in his feet to keep from pressing the gas pedal to the floor. The roads were too dangerous to drive too fast. He just needed to keep the car in sight. The roads out of town should be closed. The position between the river and the manmade lake on the other side of the road always made the main road the first to flood—and the first to be blocked off.

Pushing as far down as he could on the gas pedal, he kept his gaze locked on the taillights in front of him.

The back end of the blue car spun, then turned toward the river, plummeting down the ravine and plunging into the water.

Terror squeezed his chest. He grabbed his phone and pressed redial. The line clicked on, and he didn't wait to hear the woman's voice to speak. "Wells again. Suspect found, and the car's gone into the river. I need emergency personnel to the bridge off Main Street now."

Owen jumped out of his car and strode through the calf-high water. He had to get to her, had to save her. He couldn't lose her—not like this. Not before telling her that he loved her.

He ran as fast as he could to the river's edge. Water swarmed up the side of the riverbank, crashing against trees. Deep rivets tore up the ground, marking the path of the tires to the river. Waves washed over the top of the car, reaching out like strong arms to force it to the bottom.

He fisted his hair in his hands. The rescue vehicle needed to get here now.

A muffled thud reached his ears. He shifted his gaze over the surface of the water. *Come on, Marie. Get out of there.*

Her dark hair and oval face came into view. Relief shot through him.

She sputtered and bobbed along with the current, the water slamming against her as it carried her further from him.

He jumped in, his body numb from the cold rain and fear. The current tried to pull him under, but he fought the raging rapids. He had to get to Marie.

She turned toward him with wide eyes. She reached out her hands, breathing heavy. A wave swelled over her, dragging her under the water.

Sucking in as much air as his lungs allowed, he dove beneath the surface. The mud and debris made it difficult to see. The tangled strands of Marie's long hair flowed in his direction. He secured his arm around her waist. His lungs burned and his muscles ached, but he kicked his feet with all his strength. He broke through the surface, pulling Marie up with him, then swam for the riverbank.

Gasping for air, he dragged her motionless body to the muddy ground. He felt her pulse and almost collapsed with relief when her weak heartbeat throbbed against his fingers. He rolled her on her back, wiped the sopping hair from her pale face, and sealed his lips on hers. He breathed his air into her then pumped his hands over her chest. Sirens wailed in the distance.

Her eyes remained closed, her pulse slow and thready.

Owen kept working, kept going through the motions even as his heart splintered. "Marie! Stay with me! Help is coming."

Her chest spasmed beneath his hands, her mouth slack and her eyes sealed shut.

22

A dull ache pulsed behind Marie's closed eyes. The desire to keep her eyelids sealed shut almost beat the need to know who clasped her hand and whispered in her ear. She opened her eyes and blinked several times, taking in her surroundings.

A soft glow filtered in from the uncovered window across the room. A steady *beep, beep, beep* beat along with the rhythm of her heart—a monitor measured her heartbeat and who knew what else. The heavy smell of antiseptic would have clued her into where she was if the medical equipment hadn't.

Turning her free hand, she studied the IV that pierced her vein. Dizziness floated in her brain, and she shifted her gaze from the tubing to see who clung to her other hand.

Owen sat in a chair next to her hospital bed. His fingers nestled between hers, and he rested his chin on his forearm that nuzzled along her side. He grinned, flashing his adorable dimples, and stared into her eyes. "You're awake."

Alarm shot through her, making the machine beside her beep like a slot machine. "Where's Nora?"

"She's at the shelter with Laura and Mrs. Collins. Safe and sound."

Gratitude tightened her aching chest. Nora was in good hands. She licked her dry lips and cleared her throat. "What time is it?" The words burned her esophagus. "Is there any water?"

Owen leaned toward a small table beside him and grabbed a plastic cup. He angled the straw toward her mouth. "It's morning. You were brought here last night. You fell asleep as soon as we got you settled in a bed."

She sipped and the room-temperature water tasted as good as ice-cold liquid from the Rockies. Leaning back against the plump pillow, she studied the red scratches slashed across his stubbled cheek. "What happened to your face?"

Owen skimmed the tips of his fingers against the shallow gashes and shrugged. "Just a few nicks from the debris in the river. I'm fine."

Moisture filled her eyes. "You saved my life."

Owen lifted their joined hands to his lips and kissed her knuckles. "I thought I'd lost you. I've never been so damn scared in my life."

Marie sprang up from the pillow and winced. Her muscles pulled and tightened, and pain stabbed into her ribs. "Renee? Is she okay? Is Bill dead?"

"Your sister's here—she's fine." Owen tilted his head toward a reclining chair on the other side of the bed. "You need to relax. You're pretty banged up."

Marie swiveled her stiff neck in the opposite direction.

Renee laid curled in a ball in what had to be the most uncomfortable sleeping chair known to man. The top of the chair lay flat, almost to the tiled floor, barely wide enough to fit her sister's slim frame. Soft snores floated from her slightly opened mouth, and the mark on her eye was like a punch in the gut.

Closing her eyes, Marie sank back against the semi-raised bed. "He hurt her. I should have done more to protect her."

"You sacrificed yourself," Owen said. "And now you're both safe. Bill can't hurt you anymore. Divers went down to the submerged car at daybreak. He didn't survive the crash."

Relief seeped into her pores, followed by a pinch of guilt for feeling even an ounce of joy at someone else's death. She inhaled a deep breath and opened her eyes again. "My memory from after the crash is a bit hazy. Did I tell you what Bill said about Patricia?"

Owen tightened his jaw and nodded. "Some, but it was enough to secure a warrant last night. What we found, as well as Damon Silas' statement, put her behind bars."

Marie tilted her head and knit together her brows. "He woke up?"

"In the middle of the night. I was here," he glanced away, and a light blush dusted his cheeks. "I talked to him. He was the one who was suspicious of Patricia when more and more supplies went missing from his classroom, and she brushed it off. Eddy also slipped information around him, and Damon started putting the pieces together. He mentioned it to Erica, who dove in headfirst to figure it all out. He feels guilty about her death. Her murder will eat him up for a while."

"It's not his fault. He didn't kill her." But Marie understood heaping on guilt based on other people's actions. Healing would come for Damon—it would just take some time.

A beat of silence pulsed between them, the reminder of her heartbeat echoing through the room, as Marie moved the pads of her fingers against Owen's hand.

His strong, steady hand.

A million thoughts raged through her mind, but she couldn't think of one word to say. The nightmare was over. Bill would never hurt her or her family again. So, why did a heavy weight of sadness press against her lungs, making it hard to breathe?

Because she didn't want to leave but had no real reason to stay.

Logic warred with emotion. She'd fallen in love with Owen, but it was too soon. Too soon to tell him and uproot her life to move to Water's Edge and hope he'd feel the same way about her one day. Especially when her mom and sister needed her.

Mom.

"Did Renee call our mom?" She couldn't help the bite of anger that lingered from her last conversation with her mom.

"Yes. Wanda wanted to come to the hospital last night, but she didn't have a way to get here."

Marie tensed. "I don't know how much more of her excuses I can handle."

For a minute she'd believed her mom had really cared about what happened to her and Renee. Disappointment crushed her windpipe. She couldn't even show up.

Owen ran a hand through his hair. "You need to talk to her."

Marie raised her brows. His uneasy tone didn't sit well with her. If her mom had gotten in trouble, or he'd found out she was using again, he'd tell her. Something else was going on, but she didn't have the strength to care. "Why?"

He shot her a half-smile. "Trust me."

Confusion engulfed her already muddled mind, but she didn't want to waste her draining energy thinking about her mom. Instead, she kept her gaze locked on his and hoped to find the answers she searched for—as if he would read her thoughts and profess his own feelings and intentions.

She sighed. "So, what do we do now?"

The heavy *thump* of a cane carried into the room, and Lewis leaned against the doorframe, Katherine behind him. "Good to see you awake, girl."

Katherine stayed close to Lewis, escorting him to the side of the bed. She shot Marie a wide grin. "I'm happy you're okay. We've all been on pins and needles. Especially Owen. We couldn't get him away from your side all night."

A smile lifted Marie's lips, and warmth spread to her toes. She slid her glance toward Owen.

His hazel eyes held her gaze, and he shrugged.

Lewis cackled and leaned the cane against the bed. "You two have had stars in your eyes since you met. You shouldn't be surprised the stubborn grandson of mine slept hunched over in a chair."

"Says the man who falls asleep in his chair every day," Owen said on a huff of breath.

Lewis clicked his tongue and focused his glassy eyes on her. "I'm glad your sister's okay. Must have been scary when she went missing."

Marie swallowed past the lump in her throat and nodded.

"I hope I get a chance to know her. Are you two staying in town for a while?" Lewis asked.

Marie fought the urge to seek Owen's gaze. "I don't know what we'll do. I haven't had much time to think about the future lately."

Lewis cupped his palm under her chin. "You just got your life back. Not everyone is so lucky. Don't waste it. Figure out what makes you happy, and fight like hell to keep it."

Watery eyes blurred her vision. Lewis was right. She didn't want to waste one more day of her life. Tomorrow would come and bring its own set of problems, but in this moment, she would live the life she wanted—be the woman she longed to be.

Lewis pushed aside a stray lock of hair and kissed her forehead. "My home is always open to you and that baby of yours, girl. You rest now but know when it's time to decide your next move, I'm here."

Emotion clogged her throat, and pressure built in her chest. "Thank you."

Lewis grabbed his cane and turned to Katherine. "All right. Get me out of this germ trap before I catch my death."

Katherine rolled her eyes and cupped Lewis' elbow. "I couldn't keep him away, and now he wants to leave. Stubborn old man." Laughter softened her words.

Marie waited until Lewis and Katherine were out the door then fixed a grin on Owen. "He's right. I don't want to waste this second chance on life."

Owen framed her face in his hands. "What would make you happy? Make you feel like you're taking full advantage of the time you have?"

She gathered all her courage and sucked in a deep breath. "I want you."

Owen leaned forward and captured her mouth in his.

Excitement erupted in her belly. The future might remain unclear, but right now she had everything she'd ever wanted.

A BLUE SKY AND WARM, bright sun created a cheery atmosphere outside the car as Owen drove through the steep hills to Marie's hometown. Inside the car was a different story.

Marie stared out the passenger window, her head pressed against the seat and her mouth in a tight line. Anxiety rippled from her in waves. Trepidation filled her core. The last conversation she'd had with her mother hadn't gone well, and now that the words she'd held inside for so long were spoken, she wasn't sure what to expect.

"Everything's going to be okay." Owen squeezed her knee.

She blew out a long breath, unconvinced. Owen had tried to persuade her to call her mom, but she hadn't been swayed. Aching muscles and a bruised body took all her focus, not to mention the constant dread squeezing her soul, knowing she'd soon leave Owen to return home. She didn't have the mental strength for another round of arguments with her mom.

All she'd wanted was to focus on taking care of Nora and spending time with Owen as she'd healed back at Safe Haven Women's Shelter. Hell, if it were up to her, she'd never leave the safe home and the wonderful women she'd met in Pine Valley —women who'd come together to lift her up and offer assistance any way they could.

"Mom will be so excited to see you and Nora." Renee bounced in the backseat.

She was either oblivious to Marie's rigid nerves or was an expert at ignoring them.

Marie didn't want to waste her limited time with Owen with her mind wrapped around her impending reunion. Pushing her anxiety down, Marie swiveled her neck in his direction and lifted the corner of her mouth. "Long-distance is going to be so hard."

"We'll be okay." Owen tightened his one-handed grip on the wheel and maneuvered down the trail that wound around the handful of trailers.

The past couple of days had been filled with sweet kisses and long nights away from him. Renee had needed Marie to calm her when the nightmares swept in at night, and Nora needed her every other second in between. Owen had been patient and understanding, two things she'd never thought she'd find in a man.

Now she'd have to say goodbye, not knowing when she'd see him again.

"That's the one," Renee squealed, thrusting her pointed finger between the two seats.

Owen stopped the car in front of a white trailer with flower boxes outside the windows and an explosion of colorful plants in a small garden by a square concrete stoop.

Shock rooted her to the seat. Her mom had actually kept alive the flowers Marie had toiled over before she left home. That was a first.

The door flung open, and her mom ran down the two steps to the manicured lawn. Her dark hair was cut in a short bob, and the green eyes, so much like her own, sparkled with unshed tears.

Marie heaved a sigh and released her seatbelt. "Here we go."

Owen grazed his fingertips against her arm. "I'm right here."

His words soothed her nerves and broke her heart at the same time. He was here now, and his presence brought her so much peace, but soon he'd head back to Water's Edge without her. Only time would tell if they could make a long-distance relationship work.

Renee jumped out of the car and ran to her mother, throwing her arms around her.

Wanda clung to Renee, tears falling from her eyes. She rocked back and forth, her lips moving as she spoke against the side of Renee's neck.

Marie stepped out of the car and waited for Owen to grab Nora's carrier before slowly approaching her mom.

Wanda kept one arm wrapped around Renee's waist and faced Marie. "Welcome home, Honey. It's so good to see you and that precious little one. I've missed so much time with her."

Marie tensed her shoulders. "Hi."

Wanda extended a hand toward Owen. "Deputy Wells. It's so nice to meet you."

He shook her hand and offered her a warm smile. "Please, call me Owen."

She shuffled her feet against the loose pebbles of the driveway. "I wish you would have called, Marie. I have so much I need to tell you. Things I couldn't say before."

Marie snorted. "We said plenty the other night. I'm not sure I can listen to much else."

Owen pressed his palm to her back. "Give her a chance. Please."

Marie cast him a hard look, then focused on her mom, mentally preparing herself for whatever lame excuse she'd concocted this time. "Just say it. I've had a rough few days and need to get Nora settled."

Wanda drew in a deep breath and closed the distance between them. She grabbed Marie's hands, and Marie fought the urge to pull away. "I know I haven't always been the best mother. I've had a hard time dealing with life, and it wasn't fair to expect you to always clean up my mess. But this time, I swear it was different."

Marie took deep breaths in through her nose to keep all the emotions brewing in her stomach from spilling from her tear ducts. "It's always different." Her voice cracked, and she dropped her gaze to her feet.

"You don't understand. This time I was working with the police."

Marie's heart galloped in her chest. "What? How?"

"I hate that Bill manipulated you, but what he saw was me selling drugs to a person the police needed to gain more information about. I agreed to work with them so I wouldn't go back to jail after the last time I got in trouble. But I couldn't say anything. Not to you or Renee. No one. But if you would have come to me about the video Bill showed you, I would have told you." Her voice caught, and she rubbed a hand over her throat. "I could have stopped all of this from happening."

Marie turned to Owen and widened her eyes. "Is she serious? Did you know this?"

Owen grimaced. "I found out the night of your accident."

"That's why you wanted me to call my mom. So she could explain."

Owen nodded.

Marie glanced back at her mom. A million questions raced through her mind, but only one mattered. "Does this mean you're clean?"

"Yes. It's been over a year. Longest I've gone since you were a child." Wanda's chest puffed.

All the tension and anger and bitterness melted from Marie's bones. She flew to her mother, wrapped her arms around her neck, and buried her face in her hair.

Renee hugged their mom from behind, connecting her hands with Marie.

Marie broke away from her family and faced Owen.

He wiped the tears from her cheeks with one hand while his other held her daughter. "I'm sorry I didn't tell you. I thought it'd be better to hear it from your Mom."

"I still can't believe it." She shook her head, and the breeze whipped her hair around her face. "I never had to leave with Bill. Never had to go through that nightmare. But at least I got Nora. I'll never forgive Bill for the pain he's caused, but I wouldn't trade having her in my life for anything."

Owen cleared his throat and rubbed a hand over the back of his neck. "I'm glad you know the truth now. Maybe things can be different for all three of you."

Marie glanced behind her, where her mom and sister had discreetly turned away, then back to him. "I want everything to be different. I'm just not sure how to make that happen."

Apprehension stole her joy. Owen was about to say goodbye and drive away. Her heart sank to the pit of her stomach.

Owen dipped his chin and caressed the side of her face. "What if you could make things different by coming back to Water's Edge with me and helping people in situations like yours?"

Marie furrowed her brow. "What do you mean?"

"I spoke with Mrs. Collins about creating an outreach

program at the women's shelter for families dealing with addiction. She loved the idea and thinks you should run it."

Marie placed a shaking hand over her heart. "Me? Why me? I don't have the training for something like that."

He clasped his hand over hers and pulled her close. "You have life experience. You have compassion and understanding. You know what these families need."

She shifted her gaze from side to side until she settled her wide-eyed stare on him. She wanted more than anything to be with Owen, but her mom and sister needed her. "It sounds like an amazing opportunity. But my family…"

Wanda and Renee flanked her.

"Your family has their own lives to live," Wanda said. "Renee will be in college soon, and I need to learn how to take care of myself. You've done more for us than I should have ever expected. Now it's time to do something for you. Build a better future for you and your daughter."

Marie held Owen's gaze, questions spinning in her mind. Excitement mounted in her chest, but she had one important issue Owen needed to clarify. "Is that the only reason you want me to come to Water's Edge? To run this new program?"

Owen chuckled. "Are you serious? I love you, Marie, and I've loved Nora from the moment I set eyes on her. I want you both by my side, outreach program or not. But I want more for you than just moving in with me so we don't have to deal with a long-distance relationship. I want you to have everything you ever dreamed of."

Joy filled her soul, and a wide grin took over her mouth. "Move in with you?"

He shrugged and flashed his adorable dimples. "Only if you're ready. I'm sure Pappy would let you live with him if you'd prefer."

Marie tossed her head back and laughed then threw her

arms around his neck. "I think the world of your grandpa, but I don't want to live with him."

"Is that a yes?" Owen asked, worry shining from his eyes.

Marie pulled back and locked her gaze with his. "That's a hell yes. I love you, Owen."

Marie's heart filled with happiness, and she pressed her lips to his. Her life had taken a lot of twists and turns but had finally led her down a trail to happiness—it led her to Owen.

EPILOGUE

Owen parked in front of the Safe Haven Women's Shelter and jogged around the hood of his car to open Marie's door. Anticipation zipped through him, and he curled his hands into balls to keep them from trembling. She slid him a glance and a confused smile as she secured her hand in his and stepped out of the car.

"I thought we were going to dinner?" She smoothed her burnt orange cardigan over her floral dress. "I'm a little over-dressed for work, and even managed to get a sitter for the night."

He tugged her hand and led her through the front door, not saying a word.

The past six months, Marie had taken her idea and his resources and created an outreach program for families and friends dealing with drug-addicted loved ones. Laura and Mrs. Collins had decided to turn the carriage house in the backyard of the shelter into a designated space for Marie to use however she wished. They'd kept their project a secret, and he couldn't wait for Marie to see.

Pride pumped through him as he ushered Marie to the back

of the old Victorian house. She'd done this—she'd worked day and night on concepts and ideas with professional counselors and social workers until the surrounding area buzzed with anticipation. Marie helped serve his community in a way he'd never imagined.

Walking along the red brick sidewalk, their footsteps echoed into the crisp, fall air. The scent of fresh cut grass and the wildflowers planted at the back of the shelter hung heavy in the air. He opened the white gate and ushered her into the backyard.

Sweat coated his palms, and nerves danced in the pit of his stomach. Marie deserved perfection. She'd swept into his life like a hurricane and changed it for the better. Gave him a family he'd craved for so many years. Being a father to Nora was sweeter than he could have ever imagined, and he'd be grateful every day of his life he'd been given the privilege of watching her grow.

Rage still burned his veins at the thought of Bill and the pain Marie endured at his hands. But it'd brought her and Nora to him, and he'd do what he could every day to make them feel loved and cherished.

If Marie let him.

Owen halted in front of the two-story carriage house that matched the green and buttercream siding of the shelter. He captured both of Marie's hands in his and turned her toward him. "I still can't believe how much my life has changed since I met you."

Marie laughed. "Tell me about it."

His smile deepened. "You've not only shown me what true love is, but you've opened your heart to my family and my town. You've created this amazing space where people feel safe."

A light blush stained her cheeks, and she tilted up one corner of her mouth. "I just helped. I couldn't have done any of this without you and a whole team of professionals. Not to mention Mrs. Collins, Laura, and Sadie for keeping me sane and helping me take care of Nora."

Owen shook his head, and his chest tightened. "Don't sell yourself short. I don't know if I'll ever be able to express how proud I am of what you've accomplished."

Marie wrinkled her nose and the blush deepened to crimson.

He chuckled. He loved how his praise embarrassed her. After all she'd accomplished, she was still modest. "But that's not all you've done. You've also opened my eyes to what I'd been missing in my life. I always thought I needed to keep my walls up, keep people at a distance. I didn't want my job, or the situations I encountered, to hurt someone I loved. You broke through those walls and showed me how empty my life was. You let me play a part in raising your beautiful daughter. I love you so damn much, Marie." His throat thickened around all the emotion swirling inside him.

Marie tilted her head to the side, tears misting in her eyes. "I love you, too. It's crazy how something so horrible can bring so much good to your life if you let it."

"Absolutely, and you and Nora are the best things that's ever happened to me. I want to spend the rest of my life giving you both as much love and happiness as you give me every day. I want to be Nora's father. I want to be your husband." Owen released one hand, pulled a ring box from his pocket, and dropped to one knee. "Marie Robinson, will you marry me?"

Marie gasped. "Are you serious?"

Owen grinned and shook the ring box. "One hundred percent."

A little yelp escaped Marie's wide-open mouth, and she threw her arms around his neck. "Yes, I absolutely will marry you."

Happiness so intense swept over him, he almost fell to the

ground. He wrapped his arms around Marie and held her close, before pulling her to her feet. "Do you want to see the ring?"

She held out her left hand, and he slipped the princess-cut diamond on her finger. "It's beautiful!"

The doors to the carriage house flung open, and Pappy cleared his throat. "Are you two going to take all night? Get on in here."

Marie pressed her hand to her mouth. "What did you do?"

People from the town filled the space. Marie had come to mean just as much to them, and Owen wanted them to celebrate their engagement. Streamers and balloons whipped around, children tugging them and weaving between the adults as everyone laughed.

Damon Silas and Mrs. Jones—Eddy's mother—stood together, their smiles actually reaching their eyes.

A well of joy and gratitude sprang from his toes. Marie had not only given a place of hope for so many people in sad situations, but also provided a place for the grieving to transform their sorrows into guidance.

Turning toward all the familiar faces, Owen raised Marie's left hand in the air. "She said yes!"

Marie giggled and cheers erupted. Marie flashed her ring.

Pappy clamped a hand on Marie's shoulder and grinned. "Welcome to the family, girl. Now you'll never get rid of us."

Marie wrapped him in a hug. "I think I can handle that."

Katherine rushed forward, Mike and Tommy behind her.

Renee ran through the crowd, tugging her mom along with her, and bounced on her toes in front of Marie. Nora wiggled and giggled in Wanda's arms, her dark hair curling around her chubby face. Renee grabbed her hand and studied the ring. "I'm so excited! I get to be the maid of honor, right?"

Marie glanced up at Owen, tears running down her face. "You thought of everything."

Owen secured his arm around her shoulder and nuzzled

his mouth against her ear. "You deserve the world. Thank you for everything you do. I can't wait to make you my wife."

Marie rested her head on his shoulder. "I can't believe all these people are here for us. I never thought I'd belong anywhere, never felt like I was truly home."

"You and Nora belong with me, Marie. Always and forever."

You won't want to miss single mom Sadie's journey to true love with Deputy Tommy Wells in this heartwarming romantic suspense. Check out Sadie's Guarded Harbor today!

ACKNOWLEDGMENTS

If you fell in love with Pappy, I hope you'll be pleased to know this book was inspired by a man very much like him. Lewis Gandee, my husband's grandfather, sparked the idea for this story when he teased me about how no one would want me if I escaped danger and ran along the riverbed. A conversation that still makes me laugh to this day.

Lewis loved me like a granddaughter from the start, and he'll always have a special place in my heart. He was ornery and loving and stubborn. He lived for his family and was the best Pappy my kids could have ever asked for. I'm glad a part of him will live forever in these pages.

A big thanks to my husband and children. You always support and encourage me. Thanks to my awesome critique partners, Samantha Wilde and Julie Anne Lindsey. I couldn't survive a day without your insight and friendship.

Much gratitude to The Editing Soprano for making my words shine, and for the team at Deranged Doctors for designing another beautiful cover.

And mostly, to all my readers. I hope you enjoyed Marie and Owen as much as I did!

Until next time!
Danielle

ABOUT THE AUTHOR

Danielle M Haas is a stay-at-home mom turned author. When she isn't writing fast-paced romantic suspense novels with mysteries to live for and romance to die for, she's busy being a taxi driver to her two busy kids and forcing her introverted self to talk to other soccer moms. Her kids and husband are her world, which is also shared with her hyper Bernie doodle, mini Whoodle, and two sassy cats. Her days are packed with cuddles, kisses, and a brain constantly thinking of new ways to create danger and romance for her next book.

Sign up for Danielle's NEWSLETTER to stay up to date with everything she has going on.

ALSO BY DANIELLE HAAS

Safe Haven Women's Shelter

Laura's Safe Haven

Injured Heroes Series

Crossroads of Revival

Crossroads of Revenge

Crossroads of Delusion

Crossroads of Redemption

Crossroads of Obsession

Crossroads of Betrayal

Crossroads of Innocence

Code Name: Gemini (A Zodiac Tactical/Injured Heroes Crossover)

Murders of Convenience

Matched with Murder

Booked to Kill

Driven to Kill

The Sheffield's Series

Second Time Around

A Place In This World

Coming Home

Stand Alones

Bound by Danger

Girl Long Gone